Harry Willard French

Through Artics and Tropics

Around the World by a new Path for a new Purpose

Harry Willard French

Through Artics and Tropics
Around the World by a new Path for a new Purpose

ISBN/EAN: 9783337194024

Printed in Europe, USA, Canada, Australia, Japan

Cover: Foto ©Andreas Hilbeck / pixelio.de

More available books at **www.hansebooks.com**

THROUGH ARCTICS AND TROPICS

Around the World by a New Path
For a New Purpose

BY

HARRY W. FRENCH

Author of "Our Boys in India" "Our Boys in China"
"Our Boys in Ireland," etc.

FULLY ILLUSTRATED

BOSTON
D LOTHROP COMPANY
WASHINGTON STREET OPPOSITE BROMFIELD

TO

THE FRIENDLIEST FRIEND

OF THE WHOLE JUVENILE WORLD

AND MY FRIEND

Mrs. Y. A. Adams

THIS BOOK IS GRATEFULLY PRESENTED

CONTENTS.

CONTENTS.

CHAPTER IX.

CHAPTER X.

CHAPTER XI.

CHAPTER XII.

CHAPTER XIII.

CHAPTER XIV.

CHAPTER XV.

CHAPTER XVI.

CHAPTER XVII.

LIST OF ILLUSTRATIONS.

THROUGH ARCTICS AND TROPICS

Around the World by a New Path, for a New Purpose

CHAPTER I.

A STRANGE DISCOVERY.

"WELL, what do you make out?" Captain Downing called impatiently, to a man with a glass, clinging to the weather rigging, a little below the masthead, on the brig *Louise*.

"It's a steamer's boat, sir," the man replied. "I can't get the name. There's the likes of an oar run up for'ard, with a bit of a rag on the end of it. It's a signal of distress, sure, sir; but I can't make out any sign of life aboard."

"All right; that'll do," called the captain. To himself he muttered, "I suppose we'll have to overhaul her" — much as if it were a duty he would shirk at that moment if he could. Then aloud, he added, "Port your helm; put about and run her down."

The stanch fishing brig *Louise*, lying off the Newfoundland Banks during a gale of wind, hove to, came about, took the wind, and dashed away toward the flag of distress that was drifting in the heavy sea.

As the sailors were prepared to lower a boat the captain called for a volunteer crew to man it, and Scott Campbell and Royal Sargent, two stalwart boys of seventeen, were the first to fall into line.

They came from the same town as Captain Israel Downing. He had known them from the cradle. They had sailed with him since they first trod the deck, and he was ready to trust them anywhere.

They were orphan boys whose fathers had died at sea, and were only related by ties of the warmest, life-long friendship, but hand in hand they had gone to school, and now they were fighting their way together, into that same field of hardship and adventure where their fathers and their grandfathers had lived and fought and died.

The boat was lowered. Four sailors pulled the oars, another stood in the prow, and the second mate held the tiller rope. They had hardly touched the water when the word was given and they pulled away for the drifting boat tossing to and fro in its mute appeal for sympathy.

It was a fair-sized row boat. They could easily make out an oar, thrust into the mast-hole forward, made fast with an end of rope, bearing some poor fellow's shirt, swinging as the boat swung on the heavy sea, waving, still, the flag of distress, for some unfortunate human being.

Loose ends of rope hung over the side, lapping the water as the boat tossed about, but even now there was no sign of life.

"Stand by with the boat-hook, Mike," the mate said solemnly.

"Aye, aye, sir," replied the man in the prow, in the same low voice, for distress at sea touches every sailor's heart.

It was a moment of intense excitement for Scott and Roy. They had never before been so near to the reality of suffering, though from their earliest cradle songs to the latest sailor's yarn, their lives had been filled with the romance of distress.

Sitting with their backs to the boat they could not see it, and they were too well drilled to look over their shoulders while pulling an oar. They heard Mike's boat-hook as it caught the drifting boat, however, and a moment later it came alongside. They rested on their oars and all eyes were fixed upon the boat, but no one spoke, for there in the bottom lay three dead bodies, and stretched across them the body of a man who evidently was still alive, though entirely unconscious. The mate leaned over him for a moment; then taking the boat in tow they returned as quickly as possible to the brig.

The *Louise* returned to the Banks and the fishing continued. One gang would fish all day with lines or seines and another, on board the brig, was kept busy cleaning the fish; dumping the livers into great tanks prepared for the purpose on the deck, scraping the bodies and throwing them down into the hold, where they were packed in salt to keep them till they came to port, where they could be dried.

SCOTT'S BOAT IN LUCK.

Down in the cabin the rescued man lay between life and death.   He had recovered consciousness, but there was little hope that he could live.

One afternoon Scott was on duty watching the gauge.   It was in a sort of bulkhead, directly under the cabin where the sick man lay, and in fair weather, for light and ventilation a hatch was removed, under the bunk, leaving only a wooden grating in the floor.

From his position just under this grating Scott could not avoid hearing every word that was spoken in the cabin, and while he watched the

CLEANING THE COD.

gauge the poor fellow above him told a story to the captain that at once became so intensely interesting to Scott that he could not have forced himself to lose a single word, even if he had realized that he was over-hearing what was not intended for him.

The man said he was an officer sent from Russia to find a family named Lester.   Seventeen years before a man, James Lester, officer on an American vessel, while at Sebastopol married the daughter of a

wealthy Russian, against her father's will. He disowned her, and she
sailed for America with her husband. A year later a daughter was born
and the husband died. Nothing further was known. In the mean-
time the Russian father's remaining child had died, and recently upon

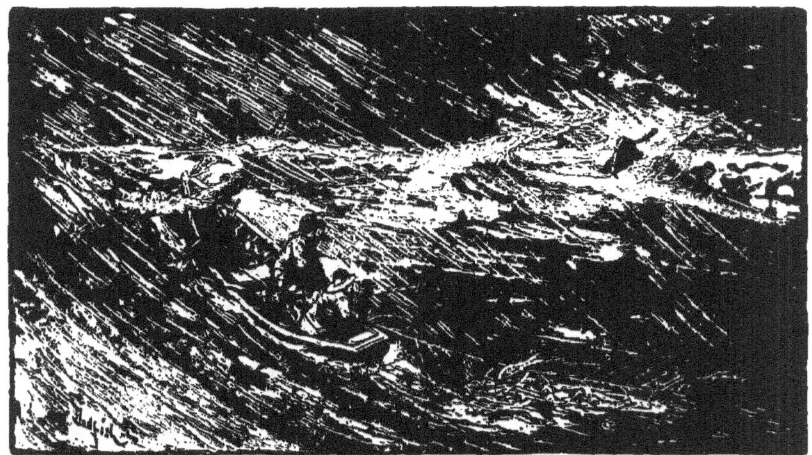

CODFISHING.

his own deathbed he willed his immense fortune to this granddaughter.
Supplied with the necessary papers, the officer had come to find the girl,
to take her to Russia to prove her identity and receive her property.
The steamer upon which he sailed was burned at sea, and with the other
unfortunates in the rescued boat he had made a struggle for life.

Captain Downing took the papers, promising to keep them safely, and
carry him at once to the person whom he sought.

Then all was still in the cabin and Scott sat watching the gauge and
thinking. It was one of those strange coincidences where the driftwood
on Life's ocean is driven right where it is required. Not far from the
house which sheltered Scott when he was on shore, in the bleak little
sea-beaten village, there lived a widow, Mrs. James Lester, with an only
daughter, Vera, sixteen years old. Scott well remembered being told
that she was named for her grandmother, who was a Russian. And

now, unless he was dreaming — and he was as sure as sure could be that
he was not — Vera Lester was to receive an immense fortune.

In the timid, modest fashion of the wild coast Scott thought of Vera
as the prettiest, the sweetest, the dearest girl in all the world, and Vera as
she wandered among the pines and white birches growing on the bluff,
accompanied by an old and almost blind Siberian hound, would stand
looking away over the water, surging in angry waves, or glistening and
flashing in the sun, thinking of that same strong, handsome sailor-boy.

Now it suddenly occurred to him that if Vera should go to Russia,
to be a great lady, she would never care what might become of him,

PACKING THE CODFISH.

Scott was glad for Vera, however, and the moment he was relieved
he hastened to tell Roy all that he had overheard.

Captain Downing's wife was dead and his only child, Louise, for
whom the brig was named, lived with her grandmother, in one of

the largest houses in the village. Roy thought as much of her as Scott
thought of Vera, and the four had always been the best of friends.

Captain Downing was a stern officer, and the boys did not venture
to tell him what they knew; but Roy as he sat by his bunk mending

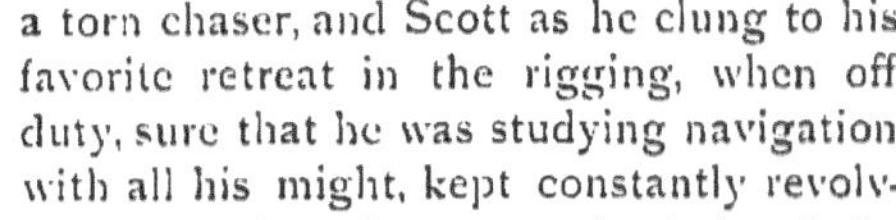

a torn chaser, and Scott as he clung to his
favorite retreat in the rigging, when off
duty, sure that he was studying navigation
with all his might, kept constantly revolv-
ing the matter in their minds,
feeling as happy, for Vera, as
though the immense fortune
were falling to themselves.

A few days later the stranger
died, and with the limited pos-
sibilities of the brig was buried
off the coast of Newfoundland.

The event cast a gloom over
the superstitious sailors. Bad
weather set in and luck seemed
entirely to have left them, so
that every one was glad when the cap-
tain set sail for home, saying that he
would sell out the catch as it was and
return in time for another haul, if fort-
une favored him.

Vera and Louise were glad to have the boys at home again, even for
a few days, for it is dull enough in such a village when all the men are
on the sea. They put on their best clothes, and Scott and Roy dressed
as though they never had been sailors, and with games and picnics the
days flew swiftly that had dragged so slowly before. But the boys had
a burden upon their minds that, from being a pleasure at first, became a
tormenting pain with long keeping.

Day after day they waited and wondered why Captain Downing did
not tell the good news to Mrs. Lester, when they would tell the girls
how they had known it all the time.

One afternoon Roy borrowed a boat of one of the neighbors, and
while the skipper lay smoking in the prow, he and Louise sailed up
and down the bay.

VERA LOOKING OUT TO SEA.

Had it not been for the presence of the skipper, Roy thought what a glorious opportunity to have whispered the secret to Louise; and he lived to regret very bitterly that he let the opportunity slip away. He even opened his mouth to speak, but noticing that the skipper was watching him he said nothing.

"To-morrow I will tell her," he thought, forgetting that "to-morrow" is a day that never comes; and many a thrilling adventure and thousands of miles of space intervened between that hour and the next time when he was able to speak to the little girl beside him.

Not long after daylight the next morning, while Roy was still dreaming of floating about somewhere, with Louise, Scott burst into his room and catching him up by the shoulder, cried:

"Roy! Roy! wake up! Captain Downing has sailed with a cargo of salt and provisions and taken Louise with him!"

"Great Scott!" exclaimed Roy, sitting up in bed and rubbing his eyes. "Scott Campbell, if you're yarning"—

"I'm not yarning, this weather, Roy. There's too big a sea on for me to set that sail. I tell you

SCOTT CAMPBELL.

the brig has been gone three hours and more. Louise's grandmother came over to see if I was aboard. She's scared to death. She says Captain Downing came home about midnight last night, and said he was going to start for the Banks on the night-tide and take Louise with him, and he did, in spite of the old lady."

"Have they really gone?" asked Roy.

"What in the world have I been telling you?" cried Scott.

"Gone without telling Mrs. Lester?"

"Yes; and it looks to me like ugly business."

" How?"

" Why, it's this way. You know he didn't dream that any one knew
of it but himself and that dead man. He has been at home ten days
without saying a word to a living soul about it. Now he's off again be-
tween two days, and nobody knew he was going. It's the first time since
we could haul a rope that he hasn't taken us with him. He's taken a
crew of only eight men and all strangers from the craft that came in with
a leak last night. He took Louise out of bed, without her knowing any-

THE DAYS ON SHORE.

thing about it, and carried her down to the brig. That's a queer kind of
crew and cargo for codfishing on the Banks."

" If he hasn't gone daft, what in the name of wonder is he up to?"
Roy asked deliberately.

" Do you want me to tell you what I think?" said Scott, stuffing his
hands hard into his pockets and leaning back against the wall.

" 'Course I do, Scott. Fire away. I guess I'm wide enough awake to understand."

" Do you suppose he could take Louise over there to Russia and make folks think she was Vera, and get that money ?"

" I more think he's gone stark mad," said Roy, deliberately clasping his hands about one bare knee, for he was much calmer by nature than

THE SKIPPER WAS WATCHING HIM.

Scott. " In the first place, salt would be a mighty poor cargo to take to Russia, unless he did it for a blind. I reckon he's very short for ready money, too, and I don't believe he could go far away from his brig if he had to pay his own expenses ; and when all's said and done he's not in Russia yet, by a very large majority, even if he's headed that way, and it's Louise he's got with him and not Vera. If he does go there, and tries to make that girl pretend she's some one else, and cheat another girl, he'll find he's everlastingly out of his reckoning, every day of the week, or I don't know Louise Downing." Then, very deliberately, Roy began to dress.

There was evidently something wrong, however, and the boys at once consulted Mrs. Lester.

CHAPTER II.

THE result of the interview was perplexing. Mrs. Lester admitted the truth of the story of her life, which no one in America knew, as her husband died shortly after Vera was born, leaving her only the low-roofed cottage which she had never seen, the Siberian hound which she had taken with her, a little puppy from her home, and the baby Vera. In circumstances so changed she had preferred to remain unknown. She could not find a box of jewels which she had always carefully treasured, which she brought from home, nor could she find her marriage certificate, but she refused to believe anything wrong of her neighbor Captain Downing, and requested the boys to let the matter drop. She even made them promise not to speak of it to any one, but they went away more convinced than ever that they were right, and that Captain Downing was wrong.

"Scott," said Roy, "we haven't much to work with, but we've got our hands and feet and heads, and maybe we can accomplish something by ourselves. If he's gone mad, Louise is in bad weather and ought to have help. If he's cheating, Vera will suffer if we don't lend a hand. But we want to get our bearings before we set our helm. Suppose you cruise round town and find out all you can, and I'll borrow Dick Rhodes' fishing boat, stock her for two or three days, and see if I can overhaul anything coming from toward the Banks that may have sighted the *Louise*."

"I'll do it," said Scott, and grasping Roy's hand for a moment, turned to his new work as a sort of detective, with a success that thoroughly alarmed him, while Roy went out to sea.

He found that the moment the brig reached the wharf, Captain Downing disposed of his cargo for cash; that he purchased a cargo of salt and large stock of provisions on credit, saying he had promised to carry supplies to several of the bankers that were running short; that he had mortgaged his house and farm for all that he could raise, and had even mortgaged the brig. By accident, Scott also learned that he had procured many sworn statements concerning Vera and her mother, and other incidents which left no doubt as to what his intentions were.

The barometer had been steadily falling while he worked, and the wind and sea were rising. Scott slept but little the second night. He was too anxious about Roy. He wished him safe on shore again.

The third morning the barometer was lower than ever, and such a tempest was howling along the coast as had never been known by the oldest dwellers by the sea.

Dense fog was hurled in heavy clouds from the ocean, completely engulfing the little town. The wind roared in a furious hurricane and

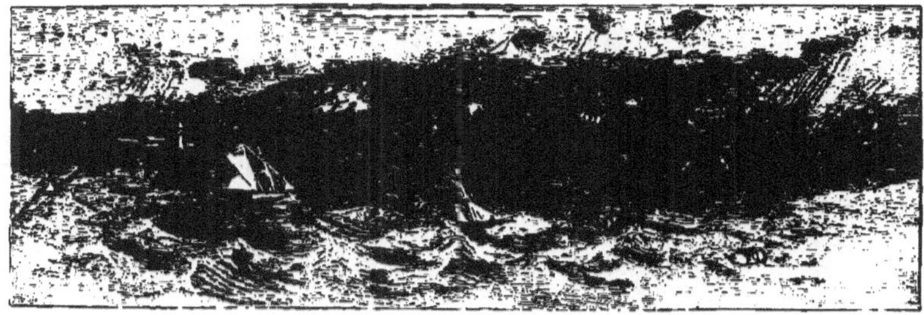

ROY BEGINS HIS SEARCH.

the wild waves dashed over the stone pier, hurled themselves fiercely among the ragged ledges on either side and even flung their salt spray defiantly against the doors and windows of the nearest cottages.

Scott was out with the earliest daylight, clad in his oil coat and hat, looking for Roy. Laboriously he made his way along the pier where a few of the villagers kept him company; such as had a father, husband, brother or son on some of the nearer fishing grounds. It was a sad and anxious company, and Scott was sad and anxious, too. He knew that Roy could handle a boat as well as any one on the coast, but he had gone into deep water with a frail craft. Scott shuddered as he looked out over the foaming sea and muttered between his teeth: "No yacht

THE LITTLE HARBOR LEDGE IN FAIR WEATHER.

that floats, with the best sailor who ever hauled a rope, could weather this gale an hour. If Roy has not found shelter he is lost."

As the day wore on the storm increased, and a larger company of anxious watchers gathered on the pier. Few words were spoken, and the answers were few and short. It was impossible to hear above the roar of the tempest unless one shouted, and there was little to say that was important enough for that. When a wave rose fiercer and higher than the rest and dashed itself over the pier and about their feet, and the wind hurled its burden of blinding spray into their faces and lashed the protruding abutments of the wharf, a groan rose from that solemn company, coming from the depths of every heart that was beating there.

Suddenly that silent crowd was roused to the most intense excitement, and the cold blood was sent throbbing through their veins. The boom of a cannon sounded. The last cry for help, from some ship in distress. It was close at hand! It shook the pier! The people, all life and earnestness now, pressed out to the end of the wharf, regardless of the breakers dashing toward them and often gurgling about their feet.

The rain was falling in torrents now, cutting away the fog, and a moment later, as another peal thundered its call for help, a huge black outline could be faintly seen, floundering and rolling helplessly among

RUSHING TO THE WEATHER RIGGING.

the waves, plunging onward before the gale toward a ragged ledge, upon the other side of the wharf, which in fair weather formed a breakwater to protect the little harbor, but to-day meant inevitable death to anything approaching it.

In fifteen minutes that vessel would be drifting past the wharf, not five hundred feet away. In half an hour it would be dashed to pieces upon that ledge.

Could nothing be done to save it? Brave men looked helplessly at each other.

Lives! human lives! Fathers! brothers! sons! Women and chil-

A HUGE, BLACK OUTLINE.

dren, too, perhaps, were there. Should they stand still and see them drift to destruction before their very eyes?

One boat was on the pier. It could not live a moment in that sea, but in the agony of their desire the men and women seized it, and pushed it into the water. The first wave dashed it against the stonework, the next splintered it from stem to stern, and the third, with a mocking roar, threw the pieces back again upon the pier.

Once more the men looked at each other, and the women clung to their helpless arms as another boom came from the drifting wreck.

Only one mortal moved upon the pier. He came running from the storehouse with a huge coil of small rope slung over his shoulder. He threw it down, quick as thought tore off his clothes, thrust his arms through a loop in the rope so that the end was held fast behind his head, and stood, for one instant, looking calmly down into a great gully, glistening and black, between two monstrous waves, upon the lee side of the stone pier. Then he turned to an old sailor who stood nearest him and shouted:

"Pay her out, steady and free! Have a cable ready for the end if I get there, and tell Roy Sargent where I went if I don't come back."

The sailor's hand was stretched out to restrain him from such madness, but he saw it coming, and with one bound sprang into the angry breakers, as far as possible from the pier.

The old sailor caught up the rope and paid it out, inch by inch, but his bronzed face was white and his strong hands trembled. Wave after wave mounted the wharf and curled about his feet, but he did not notice them. The

"PAY HER OUT, STEADY AND FREE!"

wind shrieked and the rain poured in torrents in his face, but his eyes never left the rope for one instant. Now it drifted back a little on an incoming wave, and with a shudder he drew it in. Then it would glide out again, and with a sigh he aided it to slip freely through his fingers.

"Has some one gone?"

"Is some one swimming for the wreck?"

"Swimming in that sea?"

"Who is it?"

"Who has dared?" came in gasps from pale lips, as trembling figures crowded again to the end of the pier, or stood shuddering and shaking their heads about the old sailor, whose only reply was:

"Scott Campbell is swimming to the wreck," and one and another, as the word passed from lip to lip, muttered:

"God help him!"

For an instant some one would catch a glimpse of brown hair or a white arm as the boy rose on a smaller wave, and eagerly pointing it out the crowd would try to cheer; but the cheer died in a groan as the next great wave swept over it, and their hearts stood still lest the boy should never live to come out on the other side.

Thus eleven minutes passed that seemed like a lifetime, and the old sailor still paid out. The black hulk, rolling, floundering, plunging on, was almost abreast the wharf. Those who

THE OLD SAILOR.

had brought glasses with them would hastily wipe the salt spray from the lens and for a moment catch a glimpse of sailors clutching the weather rigging, clinging to rope ladders, climbing higher and higher in a desperate struggle to get away from the surging breakers which swept the deck below.

They had fired their last signal. They had given themselves up.

Twelve minutes! Where was that atom of white among the breakers? Trembling hands passed glasses from one to another. No one could find it. It seemed an hour since they had seen it last. Had Scott Campbell given up? Was he gone! gone! gone! Or if he were still struggling, might they not drift past him without seeing the boy who was fighting with those angry waves to save them?

Thirteen minutes! The old sailor was upon his knees, on the very edge of the pier, bending anxiously forward, regardless of the tempest, of the excitement about him, of the waves that sometimes half-covered him. He held the rope between his thumb and finger as though it were a thread of glass. His breath came short and sharp. His eyes were riveted upon that line as it rose and fell, floating upon each incoming wave. It faltered. His brow contracted. It fell back with the next wave. With a sharp cringe he drew it in a little that it might not be fouled upon the pier. It rested there a moment. The old sailor did not breathe. It fell back again. With a groan he let his hands drop and the rope drift.

What was that? It made a sharp dart forward! It slipped from his fingers! He started, caught it in his hand, stared for an instant, then sprang to his feet, and in a voice that sounded clear and shrill above the tempest, he shouted :

"Glory to God! Stand by with the cable! Scott Campbell has reached the wreck!"

CHAPTER III.

A WILL AND A WAY.

WHEN the sun rose the next morning, the stormy clouds were drifting away from it and the waves were wearing themselves out. The great hull, black and bare, swept clean above the deck, from stem to stern had been hauled up as far as possible, stranded and made fast by strong cables, with the cargo still intact, and every soul on board safely transported to the shore ; while boisterous sea-gulls, hundreds of them, filled the air, diving and splashing in the water about the wreck, having a grand and noisy feast to welcome the returning sunshine.

The family of the owner of the vessel and cargo, a wealthy ship-owner, were on board the wreck. He had been telegraphed for and arrived in the afternoon. He sent at once for Scott, who found him sitting upon an iron bench by the door of the house where his family had taken refuge.

"Young man," he exclaimed, grasping Scott's hand — then he stopped and for a moment was unable to speak. At last he continued: "I have a very valuable cargo down in that hold, and my wife and children were on board for a summer holiday. I watched them sailing away, little thinking of this end. You saved me a great deal of money, but infinitely more you saved to me the lives of my wife and children. I can never repay you, but I beg you to let me hand you this. It is nothing. I shall try and do something more for you if I can find the opportunity." He put an envelope into Scott's hand and added, with tears in his eyes, "Be as generous as you were brave, my boy. Do not think it is given you as pay for your noble deed and scorn it as such, but for my sake make use of it, and let me know whenever I can be of service to you."

At that moment Roy came running down the road. He cleared the

fence at a bound. Scott stuffed the envelope into his pocket and in a moment forgot all about it as he clasped Roy in his arms.

The shipowner looked on in kindly admiration as Roy exclaimed:

"I've just heard all about it, Scott. What a hero you are! I always knew you were just the fellow who could do it; but there's not another man upon the coast who could."

"Or who would have dared to try." added the shipowner, eagerly.

"Let up on that, now, Roy," Scott exclaimed impatiently, and very much embarrassed. "You have doubtless heard a great deal too much about me, but I've had no chance to hear a word about you. You'd have done better than I in the same place. You always do; but go ahead now, and tell me where you've kept yourself."

THE STRANDED HULL.

"There's an account in print that blows my horn for me," said Roy, laughing and handing Scott a newspaper. "Of course it's much better than I deserve, but I never thought of being ashamed. In fact, I was rather proud of it. I was going to show it to you with a tremendous flourish, till I got in on the afternoon stage, and heard how far ahead of me you were, and that kind of took the wind out of my sails, I tell you."

"Let up, I say!" Scott exclaimed sharply, glancing from the newspaper. "Now go ahead and tell me where you have been."

Roy threw himself carelessly upon the bench and replied, in his old, deliberate way:

"Well, I was aboard Dick's boat till she was stove to smithereens. Then I was on a steamer. Can you believe it, I've walked the bridge as pilot and been paid for it, too, so I have. I was off Eagle Ledge when the storm struck in —by the way, the *Louise*

"WHEN THE STORM STRUCK IN."

did go to the Banks, but I'm pretty sure she didn't stop there. It's my opinion she took her cargo of salt to St. John's for a blind; but I'll tell you: I ran into the cove and pulled up on the rocks to wait till I could run home. You know there's a steam fog horn on the ledge and a bell buoy off the point. The fog shut down with a steamer in sight and a sail near to. Well, the bell buoy broke loose the first thing and drifted on to the rocks, half a mile above me. Then something silenced the fog horn. In the very worst of the storm it stopped working. All of a sudden I heard the steamer's fog whistle, off to windward; it was blowing and slashing like mad,

THE BELL BUOY.

and I thought if that steamer was hunting for the buoy and fog horn she was more than likely to run her nose right into the rocks. By good luck I got my boat into the water, between two waves, flung out sail enough to catch a hatful of the gale, and let her go for the steamer's whistle. In ten minutes I was in sight of her. Jehu! but she was an ocean steamer, drifting like mad dead on to the ledge. I yelled, but they couldn't hear me. They saw something was wrong, however, and lay to. and stopped her. They threw me a line, but it was no use. I saw I'd got to get on board, some way, to make them understand, for the wind alone was carrying them four or five knots an hour, so I worked round to windward. went broadside on, and when a wave slung me up against her I jumped for all I was worth. I went clean over and landed. sprawled out at full length on the deck, in a foot or more of salt water. It didn't take me long to give the captain his points, you bet.

"'Do you know this coast?' he shouted.

"'Every inch of it, sir,' I yelled.

"'Where's Sheep Island?' he asked, and a half-dozen other points in the same way, and I gave them to him quick as I could breathe.

"'Come up on the bridge,' he said, by way of winding up, and there was nothing for me but to obey, for you see Dick's boat was smashed and gone adrift. All my stores were at the bottom of the sea, and I had no money to pay my fare, so 'twas either work my passage or be put ashore to walk home. I worked it, I tell you. Oh! but it's fun being pilot, if you only had time enough to appreciate it. Coffee, soup, every

"JEHU! BUT IT WAS AN OCEAN STEAMER!"

thing, all served on the bridge, and everybody, from the captain down,
dancing about to make you comfortable. The trouble is, that the
thought that you've got a big steamer on your hands in a roaring hurri-
cane, is worse than the gale in your face for taking your wind away, and
I didn't think of anything but rocks until I was on shore again. It was
a little after dark when we sighted the island light, just as I said we
should, and as the steamer was leaking badly, the captain ran into port.
He wanted me to stay aboard till he heard from the Company, but I told
him if he'd give me enough to pay Dick for his boat and buy a ticket
home on the cars, I'd like to be
off on the night train. He said
I'd surely earned a pilot's fee be-

side, and insisted on
my taking a roll of
bills, and before I got
away the passengers
crowded round and
stuffed another roll
into my pocket. I
was so confused I
didn't know what to
do, and when I was
safely on board the

"I JUMPED FOR ALL I WAS WORTH."

cars, and counted it up, what do you think? There was over seven hun-
dred dollars! How's that for a starter toward following the brig *Louise?*
It was a great deal more than I deserved, of course, but as we passed

the light, there lay a big ship, with sails still set, high and dry upon the rocks, and I suppose the steamer folks thought they were better off out of such a predicament, even if it did cost them something."

The shipowner said good-by as he was leaving with his family, earnestly thanking Scott again, and urging him to call upon him whenever he could be of service, and the boys wandered down to the coast, still talking over their adventures, when Scott suddenly thought of the

"WE SIGHTED THE LIGHT."

envelope in his pocket. He broke the seal, and the two boys sat in blank astonishment, staring at the contents. It was a check, payable to Scott Campbell, for ten thousand dollars.

Scott's first thought was to return it, but he remembered the tears in the donor's eyes when he asked him to be as generous as he had been brave, and turning to Roy he said earnestly:

" It is a gift from God, to use in securing Vera Lester's rights. If you are with me, Roy, we'll fit out the best boat we can get, and the largest we can handle, and we'll follow Captain Downing to the end of the world."

"Over land and sea!" said Roy, grasping Scott's hand; "through Arctics and Tropics, I'm with you, Scott, till we find that Captain Downing is innocent, or force him to walk the deck as he should."

So they pledged themselves for a longer, more formidable, more exciting chase than either of them dreamed, and set themselves at once to make their preparations.

ROY'S STORY IN PRINT.

CHAPTER IV.

NO time was to be lost.   The boys borrowed a yacht, and, putting on their fishing clothes, that they might look precisely what they were, ran down the coast to the city, keeping a sharp lookout among the shipping as they entered the harbor, to see if such a craft as they wanted was there.

" Do you see that steamer over there, Scott ? " Roy asked.   " That's the one I brought in, night before last.   They've unloaded her, and are working her over to those docks there, for repairs, I guess.   She was leaking pretty bad, they said."

Coming up to the wharf, Scott sat in the boat while Roy, as the acknowledged " business man " of the little corporation, went up to make inquiries concerning several sloops and yachts which lay at anchor.

Almost the first man he met was the captain of the steamer, who grasped his hand, and at once introduced him to the manager of the line, who had come on to attend to the disabled steamer.

" I was going to hunt you up, Mr. Sargent," he said, "just as soon as I got the repairs under way.   The Company is greatly indebted to you for the service you rendered.   Now you have saved me wandering about in search of you, and I am greatly obliged to you for that, too," he added, with a pleasant smile.

Roy was so embarrassed at hearing himself called " Mr. Sargent " for the first time in his life, that he hardly knew what he said.   He tried

Mrs. Lester and Vera. The bark was hauled into open water by a tender, and as Roy and Scott rowed out in the gig to meet her and take command, Mrs. Lester waved them a God-speed from the wharf, and Vera watched until her blue eyes were so full of tears that she could see nothing but one great gleam of light.

The boys had an animated controversy as to which should command. Scott declared that the vessel was Roy's and that Roy was captain, and finally carried the day, with the agreement that Scott, as the one who was really the prime mover, should be first mate on deck, but admiral in the cabin, and should have the general direction of the voyage.

The bark was named *Snowbird.* Two of the seamen and the

MRS. LESTER AND VERA.

cook had sailed in her before, while the other two were old whalers. Their first point was the Newfoundland Banks, and the run was all that could have been wished. As they came among the codfishers, Scott took his position at the masthead to look out for the brig *Louise*, but, though they spoke several bankers, no tidings were heard from her till they came to port at St. John's, at the southeastern extremity of the island. They had both of them been on shore at St. John's before, so that their

SCOTT AT THE MASTHEAD.

eyes and thoughts were bent wholly upon business. First, they made sure that the *Louise* was not at anchor in the almost land-locked bay. Then they crossed the bay and dropped anchor, and Scott and Roy, having made the first step in safety, took the gig and rowed ashore, to the quiet, quaint, steep-roofed old town lying opposite the narrow entrance.

"St. John's looks very unlike an American city, but its hardy, hospitable people would make any one feel at home," Scott observed, as they were warmly welcomed by one and another who only knew of them that they were sailor boys.

They did not have to apply to the American consul, as they expected, for every one was ready to answer questions, and every one at St. John's seemed to know about every one else there, and every one who had ever been there.

"Yes! The brig *Louise* ran in here some two weeks ago," said one of the wharf officers. "She had a cargo of salt which she sold for cash at a low price, and took in a cargo of grain, flour and mixed stuff for two or three of the southern ports of Greenland. Captain said he had agreed to go up there and fetch back overstock from some whalers."

The boys looked at each other, but said nothing. There were a few stores which were lacking in their outfit, which must be purchased at St. John's, and while they were wandering about the quaint old streets, Scott slipped into a jewelry store, closely followed by Roy.

"What did you run into this port for?" Roy asked, and Scott, with a decided blush, replied:

"I thought we'd be writing to Mrs. Lester, from here, to tell her of our success so far, and maybe 'twouldn't be a bad idea to slip in some little trinket for Vera, just to show her that we haven't forgotten her."

"We!" said Roy, with a merry laugh. "Bet yer best anchor, Scott, Vera isn't worrying for fear that I've forgotten her. She'd know I hadn't forgotten my old playfellow."

Scott laughed too ; but he very carefully selected a little chain, with a cross attached, had it safely packed in a box and addressed. Then they took it to the post-office, registered it, and returned to the *Snowbird*.

IN THE HARBOR AT ST. JOHN'S.

They wrote a letter to Mrs. Lester and sent it on shore by two of the sailors, who were to bring back the stores they had purchased, including a lot of fresh meat. Then they sat alone in the cabin ready to lay the course to Greenland.

"I tell you what it is, Scott," said Roy, "I never dreamed what a terrible strain I was under, running up here, till the anchor dropped and we were in the gig. When I looked back and saw the *Snowbird* lying

there, all in regulation ship-shape, and realized that you and I had brought
her here, my knees began to shake, and I wondered how in the world we
ever dared to do it."

"It took me the other way," said Scott. " I knew the ground so far,

and had faith in the captain, but when I saw that big lump of ice we
passed just outside, and realized that when we went out through those
narrows again it would be by a new path, for a new purpose that would
lead us no one knows where or for how long, my knees began to shake
and, to tell the truth, they are shaking still. Roy, I wonder if I'm a
coward."

Roy laughed heartily and exclaimed, "Scott Campbell, if your knees
were shaking till you could not stand, I'd give more for the courage you
had left than for the whole stock of any two fellows on the coast."

" Royal Sargent, let up!" said Scott decidedly, "and when you come
down again, let it be to business. So Captain Downing has gone to
Greenland."

" Well, what in the name of common sense has he done that for ? "

"How should I know? You know how often he remarked that 'Doubtful things is mighty onsartin.'"

"I don't believe he's gone there at all," said Roy. "I believe he's simply gone daft."

"Yes, he has," Scott replied, who was studying a large chart spread out upon the table. "It's hardly out of his way at all, if he's doing what I think and going to Russia, for he'd have to go north of Scotland, any way, and by lugging freight he is sort of paying his way, and throwing any one off the track at the same time. He's got a lot of money with him, you know, and he's working fair and foul for more, because he'll need it."

"To say nothing of buying everything on credit and selling it for cash. It looks as though there was method in his madness, any way."

"Why not go straight to Russia and head him off?" Scott exclaimed.

"I don't believe he's going there. I believe he's parted a cable in his upper story, and I want to overtake him and save Louise," Roy replied. And Scott agreed, feeling ashamed that he had forgotten his friend's anxiety in his own. "Two points east of north and a straight course will fetch it," he said.

At that moment there was a commotion on deck, and the boys rushed up. It was after nine o'clock at night, but the sun was still shining brightly. A hawk, chasing a small bird, had flown against the rigging and dropped dead upon the deck — at the feet of one of the sailors, forward.

THE CABIN OF THE SNOWBIRD.

"Good enough for him!" Scott exclaimed, but Roy, noticing the solemn faces of the two seamen and the cook, replied in a low voice:

"But not for these superstitious sailors. They'll have it, every false wind that blows, that this was a warning."

And Scott and Roy were quite sailors enough themselves to wish that it had not happened.

"We are ten days behind the *Louise*," Scott said, as the men hauled up the anchor, and they all worked together setting sail.

"It may be twenty, or it may be more, by the time we reach Green-

A HAWK DROPPED DEAD UPON THE DECK.

land," Roy replied; and Scott, as he caught his eye, turned instinctively to the spot where the hawk fell.

A light breeze set in from the sea as they worked their way out of the narrow inlet, and the great cliffs, the wave-washed ledges and the moss-green coves of Newfoundland quickly sank into a dense fog behind them, while the moonlight still lay, white and beautiful, over the sea.

Both of the boys were serious and thoughtful that night. They had left behind them the last point of land with which they had ever been familiar. They were strangers now, in a world full of uncertainty.

The sea breeze continued and increased. Morning dawned at two o'clock, and Scott's first work on coming on deck for his watch, was to take in sail.　At night a little more sail was taken in, and the third night they were scudding along, careened almost to the water with only a single sail and jib.

They had passed several "lumps of ice" of varying size, which, to Scott and Roy, appeared to be very fair icebergs, and proved intensely fascinating, but the old sailors paid them very little attention till the third night, when one of them asked to be allowed to keep lookout watch forward.

"Why, we are bowling along beautifully," Roy remarked; "and there's not a rock between us and Cape Farewell."

The old fellow touched his hat respectfully, and said:

"We may be at a standstill, sir, before to-morrow night."

"Ice?" said Roy.

"Ice, sir," replied the sailor.

The possibility served to give the young captain a very wakeful night, but twenty-four hours

THE SNOWBIRD, THE MOONLIGHT AND THE SEA.

later found them still close hauled and still plunging forward, making nearly eight knots an hour, with the ice constantly increasing about them, and stormy petrels, with their warning cries, hovering near them.

Here and there real Arctic monsters now came bearing down upon them, rising far above the tops of their masts, and ten or twelve times longer than the *Snowbird*. They were often surrounded on the lee by a cluster of smaller bergs, while a cold gray mist settled down on the water, more treacherous than a fog, sometimes freezing as it fell, for an hour or more, making it almost impossible to stand upon the deck or handle the ropes and sails.

After an unusually long ice-rain, early on the fifth morning, it began to snow. The wind blew a gale, and the snow was so thick that it was hard to see the length of the *Snowbird*. Scott and a sailor held the helm. One sailor stood in the prow, and another sat at the masthead. Roy, one sailor and the cook, having been up all night, were sleeping, when the two lookouts, at the same instant, shouted:

"Ship ahoy! Dead ahead!"

Scott could see nothing, but at a venture put his helm hard down to port. Instantly the *Snowbird* took the hint, came

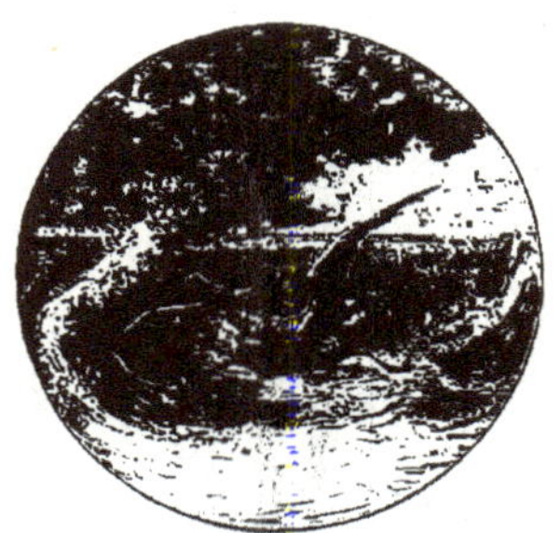

THE STORMY PETREL.

into the wind, and lay rolling upon the great waves, as a steamer, sheathed in ice and snow from trucks to water-line, passed so close that the spray from her prow was dashed in Scott's face as he stood at the helm.

They found it impossible to hold the course to the north, and fell off to the west, passing several large icebergs, glistening and gray, like frosted silver, and the air seemed as cold as at midwinter. It had become a common incident now, to bump into great lumps of ice, shaking the little *Snowbird* from stem to stern, but, thanks to the sheathing of the bows, doing no other damage.

Before the snowstorm ceased Roy came on deck, and he and Scott held a consultation with the sailor whom they had appointed second mate, that he might act as a sort of Arctic guide.

Ice anchors, cables and setting-gear were got in readiness, and none too soon, for above the roar of the tempest the ominous grinding and creaking of pack-ice could be distinctly heard, and now and then a crash like thunder announced that two great icebergs had come together at no great distance.

SHE WAS ICE TO THE TRUCKS.

An hour before sunset the alternating snow and sleet ceased alto-
gether, as suddenly as it began. But what a scene met their eyes! A
solid mass of pack-ice, far as the eye could reach, was bearing down upon
them from the open sea, while upon the port huge icebergs, surrounded
by their guards of broken ice, were moving with the tide in the very eye of
the wind. Behind them there seemed nothing but ice. How they had
ever come through it was a mystery.

Scott was at the helm. Roy stood braced against the mast. The
Snowbird tossed like a cork upon the waves ; bumping, bumping, bump-
ing against the floating ice. Here and there a rift appeared with open
water, but the position of the ice changed so rapidly that it was
impossible to take advantage of it. Upon the port bow a steamer was
pushing her way through the ice. A thousand feet away one of the

"THEY HEADED FOR THIS ICEBERG."

largest icebergs was lying, motionless, apparently, in all the tumult. Roy
talked for a moment with Scott, and they headed for this iceberg.

Fortunately the veteran seamen needed only general directions to
make fast upon the lee side of the iceberg, for the young commander,

who had never seen the operation, would have made poor work directing. He kept his eyes wide open, however, and the next time could command or take a hand himself. The berg was in the shape of an enormous mound on one side, ending in an abrupt ledge of gleaming ice on the

"ROY, AXE IN HAND."

other, while the gradually sloping side was surrounded at the base by a platform of smooth, flat ice.

No sooner had the *Snowbird* touched the berg than the men were out on the ice with ice-anchors, forward and aft, and in fifteen minutes the little bark was held so fast that she scarcely moved with the waves.

"We are surely safer here than dodging about in this gale," said Roy, and, anxious to make the most of every opportunity, the boys were soon out upon the ice.

Their first discovery was a ship's anchor, caught in the ice.

"It is the relic of some one in trouble," said Roy, "but it is heavier than ours and we may need it."

He went for an axe to cut it free, when Scott discovered a brig in the distance, dodging and tacking in the gale, trying to find a way out from among large icebergs closing in upon her.

" I'm going to take a look at her in the gig," Scott exclaimed, and before Roy could remonstrate he was pulling away over the waves, and Roy, axe in hand, stood watching the brig in its struggle and the little boat midway. It might be the *Louise*.

Scott was half-way across the open water which divided the two masses of ice when she made a desperate dash to cut her way through, failed, fell away with the ice packing behind her, careened almost to capsizing, caught the wind again and made a dash for a narrow rift between two icebergs. Even Roy, from the distance, knew better than that.

" Fools !" he muttered in his excitement. " Port your helm ! Lie to and let her come." They did not hear him, however, more than a mile away. They entered the rift between two huge icebergs that were approaching each other, because they saw clear water beyond, and it was a last extremity. The moment they were under the lee of one they lost their wind and headway. It was too late for the boats ; too late for anything. With a crash which shook the ice where Roy was standing, and echoed like the roar of cannon along the sea, the two crystal mountains plunged against each other and became one pyramid of ice, with the brig and every one on board buried in its silent heart.

The yawl was lowered from the *Snowbird*, and Roy with two seamen followed Scott, but two hours later returned without a trace of the wreck, except a deck water-cask which must have gone overboard when she careened.

The cask was marked " *Chieftain*, New York."

" So it was not the *Louise*, at any rate," said Roy, with a deep sigh.

" No, thank God," Scott added fervently. " But it has taught me a good lesson — to respect these monsters. And it makes me much more thankful than proud, to know that the *Snowbird* is still safe."

CHAPTER V.

THE sea calmed down very quickly, and the boys slept soundly, leaving the *Snowbird* in charge of the second mate, who was naturally better than either of them to watch the progress of the ice.

It seemed only a moment, and, indeed, it was less than three hours when he called them again to see the sun rise. It was a wonderful sight. A silver-gray haze hung over everything. The water was still full of ice, but it was no longer boisterous or dangerous, while the sun, piercing the frosty mist, transformed each iceberg, large and small, to a mass of tangled rainbows. The very air was full of beautiful rainbows. The larger bergs were marvelous in their gorgeous coloring. The boys left the bark, and taking several instruments and a glass with them, made their way to the top of the iceberg.

A steamer was slowly moving southward about a mile away. Scott wanted to hail her, but there was a great deal of floating ice between them, and Roy was afraid that if they made her come so far out of her way just to tell two boys if she had seen the *Louise*, the captain would be so angry he would not answer, and they let her go.

There is always a powerful fascination to the stranger in the grand sights of the Arctic Ocean, and the boys turned reluctantly to their instruments to locate their position, as this was the first time they had seen the sun for nearly four days.

"SLOWLY MOVING SOUTHWARD."

They heard the sailors down below filling the water tanks from the streams of fresh water trickling down the side of the iceberg, and were busily engaged upon their calculations, when the berg beneath them began to swing very slowly.

They started to their feet. There was a shout from below, and catching up their instruments they hurried down.

As they ran toward the bark, two of the sailors were pulling on the forward anchor and one working frantically at the rope from the stern, while the poor little *Snowbird* was pulled way over and almost capsized.

" Cut loose that aft anchor, sir ! " yelled the second mate, from the deck.

" Get on board, quick, Roy, with this thing," Scott exclaimed, handing

" IT WAS A WONDERFUL SIGHT."

Roy the instrument he was carrying and pulling his sailor's knife from his belt. Roy sprang on to the deck with his precious burden just as Scott cut the cable. It snapped with a sharp twang like the breaking of some huge violin string. The *Snowbird*, suddenly set free, slid off the ice, dove into the water, taking a great gulp of it over her bows, and shot away, out upon the waves.

Scott had no time to speculate upon his position, for the iceberg swung back once more, hesitated an instant, then with a resounding crash gave a great lurch, and ice-water of the coldest and sharpest was gurgling in his ears, blinding his eyes and rushing past him like a furious river. He realized that a part of the iceberg at least, must be on top of him bearing him down, and had just presence of mind left to put one hand over his mouth and hold his nose with the other.

When he became conscious again he was still under water, sliding rapidly in some direction along the smooth ice. He thought he was drowning, but just as he was about to give up he saw a gleam of light above him, struck out with might and main, and an instant later shot out of the water as far as his waist, with the bright sun full in his face. The iceberg was behind him. He was so benumbed by cold

SCOTT'S FIRST VIEW.

that he was hardly more than conscious, but while he struggled to keep his head above and catch his breath, he heard Roy calling:

"All right, Scott. Hold there a second. Are you hurt?"

"Guess not," he gasped, "but cold. Colder'n Greenland!"

A moment later Roy was beside him. He was too cold to help himself, and the gig was too light to pull him in, so Roy could simply hold on to him till another boat with two sailors came up.

"Jehu!" said Roy, when they had Scott at last safe in the cabin. "I wouldn't go through that for a farm Down East. I thought you were never coming up, but when you did come you popped out just like a seal. You missed a wonderful sight, I tell you. That whole iceberg, bigger than a dozen churches, just rolled right over like a lump of ice in a glass pitcher. It went right over on top of you, and I believe every particular hair on my head stood on end. I don't remember anything about starting, but the first I knew I was in the gig pulling like mad. It's lucky we left it in the water last night."

"Well, we're learning something about ice navigation, at any rate," Scott said, as he pushed his feet closer to the stove and drank a cup of hot coffee.

Just then a sailor lifted the skylight and observed: "There's a sail away to the starboard, sir, and land three or four miles to port."

"Land!" Roy gasped, springing to his feet and rushing on deck.

"Land!" Scott exclaimed, jumping into a pair of dry boots and a thick jacket and following him.

They were spinning along almost due north, in water that was comparatively clear of ice when Scott emerged. Roy was at his old position, braced against the mast inspecting a dark horizon on the port-bow, that was land and high land, too, without a doubt.

"That's Labrador, and no mistake," he observed; "and that's why we couldn't make our calculations come out any where this morning. The fact is, Scott, we've been driven more than a hundred miles off our course."

"Let's run in," said Scott, still shivering from his cold bath. "If that's

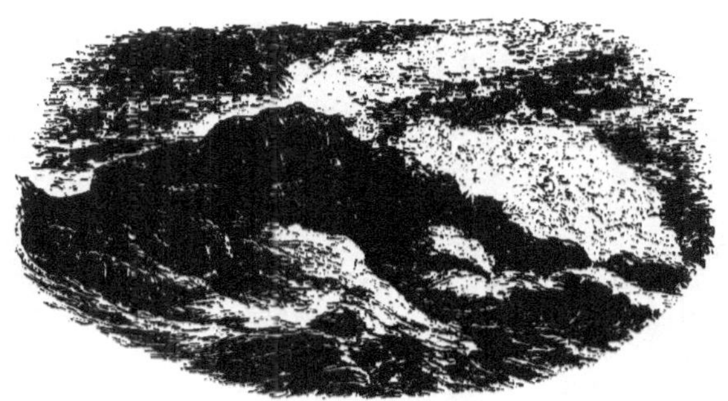

"LAND!" ROY GASPED.

Labrador it means rocks and birds. I wouldn't mind climbing over rocks for an hour after some of them, to warm up a bit."

"Nor a game dinner after it, either," Roy replied, and turning to the man at the helm he gave the order to make for the land.

"Glory!" Scott cried, as they neared the wild and savage rocks at the boldest point of Labrador, just south of the confluence of Davis and

Hudson Straits. "What if we'd been a little closer in when the storm took us!" He shuddered.

"Don't you almost wish yourself off Cape Race again, catching cod?" Roy asked, and smiled, though his face was rather pale and solemn as he watched the great waves banging against that grim ledge and tossing their spray nearly a hundred feet high.

FAT AND LAZY PUFFINS.

They left it to the second mate to select a safe fjord where they could come to anchor. Then, as they were leaving in the gig, Scott asked, "These rocks will not come loose and drop us, will they?" at which the sailors laughed heartily.

They gathered two large baskets full of eggs, and had no need of firearms in securing all that the gig could carry of the fat and lazy puffins, the penguins of Labrador. As they were returning they shot two eider ducks and half a dozen of Mother Carey's chickens.

"Those eider ducks are the handsomest birds I ever saw," said Scott, holding one in his hands as Roy pulled back to the bark. "Look at the head and back, it is white as snow. Then that crimson neck, and breast as black as coal. And there is gray, green, black and yellow, white and brown all mingled there."

Once more they set their course, this time due northeast, wishing to make the southern ports of Greenland, which were very nearly east; but to do it they must allow for the strong course of the arctic current, noted on the chart.

As they were moving out of the fjord, one of the sailors spied a huge whale lying dead upon the rocks, where he had drifted at high water, wounded by a harpoon, no doubt, from which he had temporarily escaped.

They were close upon some of the fishing grounds, and as they rounded a high promontory, late in the afternoon, with the shore still close upon the port beam, they sighted a stanch, weather-beaten whaler lying at anchor in the straits, while her boats were grappling with an

"IT MEANS ROCK AND PERIL"

enormous whale. The *Snowbird* passed within five hundred feet of them. The sailors' eyes danced, as they hung in the rigging and watched the excitement of their old trade, and Scott and Roy would willingly have taken a hand.

"'Tisn't much like landing cod, is it?" said Roy, as they turned away.

Scott was watching an iceberg. There was, however, very little ice

STRANDED.

in the water now, but a few large icebergs were constantly in sight.

" They taught us in school that there was seven times more ice under the water than out of it," he said, pointing to a monster slowly moving across their bows. " That's two hundred feet high at least, isn't it? Do you believe there's fourteen hundred feet of water under us?"

" No, nor half that," Roy replied.

" Let's throw the lead and see.   We haven't tried taking soundings yet."

" I told you so!" said Roy triumphantly, as they marked just eighty fathoms or four hundred and eighty feet, on a hundred fathom line.

"GRAPPLING WITH AN ENORMOUS WHALE."

" There's seven times more ice — only it's spread out more and solid, sir," said a sailor, and the boys looked at each other and resolved not to be quite so quick in coming to conclusions, in the face of science, in the future.

They passed a few more whalers and one or two Danish brigs, and a chunky little steamer working through the ice, but did not come in sight of land.   Three times a day they took the most careful observations, and each time seemed to be farther and farther north, while by dead reckoning, by log and compass, they should be almost in the middle of Greenland.

Again the old sailor was of value in calling to mind what they already knew but had forgotten to apply, that there was always a great variation of the compass in the far north, when the north pole and the magnetic pole

CLIMBING OVER THE ROCKS.

were in two distinctly different directions. Again the boys looked at each other in a way to indicate that they realized they had yet much to learn, and, by the sun, set their course due east.

Ten hours later the lookout reported land ahead. It was a little island with drifting ice for half a mile clinging to the lee shore. Upon this ice were seals without number, and five or six walrus. The huge fellows looked very tempting, and Scott was so anxious to have a shot at them that the *Snowbird* hove to, and he and Roy landed on the ice. There

"WORKING THROUGH THE ICE."

was a grand adjournment of the meeting as the boys approached, but finally, creeping on his hands and knees, Scott came near enough to have a fine shot at one dignified old walrus, with tusks nearly a foot long.

He took a careful aim and fired. He evidently hit, for he was a good shot, and the walrus gave a little jump. Roy said he looked as if an idea had struck him. He quietly lifted his head, looked back over his shoulder at the boys, nodded and gave a little snort, as much as to say, " You'll learn better than to waste powder on a tough-skinned fellow like me, if you try it often enough," and then quietly rolled over into the water, leaving a good laugh behind him at Scott's expense.

"A DIGNIFIED OLD WALRUS."

They still bore away to the east. Night came on, at least by the chronometer, but with the sun still shining through a brilliant haze, like a beautiful sunset, and against the bright color they distinguished sharp snow-crowned peaks, rising out of the horizon and cutting into the sky.

A SEA-LION.

"They're 'Greenland's Icy Mountains!'" Scott shouted, as Roy came up from below to take his watch on deck.

The two boys stood at the helm together for a few moments, before Scott went below.

"Aren't you rather proud, Captain Sargent?" Scott said, laying his hand affectionately upon Roy's shoulder.

"I'm very thankful," Roy replied earnestly. "Scott, what should you and I have done all alone here in a craft we two could have managed at home?"

"THEY'RE GREENLAND'S ICY MOUNTAINS!"

CHAPTER VI.

AFTER sleeping soundly for several hours, with his jumper hung over the port to keep out the sunlight, Scott was called by a sailor, who notified him that it was a half-hour before his watch on deck began.

He pulled the jumper from the port, and peering through the thick green glass obtained his first glimpse of real Greenland. At a little distance was a man in a tight-fitting skin shirt, bareheaded, with a face almost the color of coffee, sitting in a canoe completely covered in with skins, sewed together and stretched over a light wood frame. He had thrust himself through a small hole in the top, up to his waist, and drawn the sides of the opening so tight about him that not a drop of water could get in. The waves dashed over him, but he did not mind them. He might have capsized and righted a dozen times without difficulty.

Before him was a small skin-covered barrel, to help him right the canoe, and behind him a reel, upon which a strong cord of seal or walrus skin was coiled, the end of which was made fast to a harpoon which he held in one hand, while with the other he used a double-bladed paddle, darting about over the waves and through them, like a fish.

Just as they were passing out of sight a huge sword-fish rose. The canoe leaped forward till its bow almost touched the shining back. The harpoon flew through the air, sank into the side of the fish and disappeared with him as he dove.

the oomiak, or woman's boat, completing Greenland's naval architecture.

When Scott reached the deck, the *Snowbird* was beating her way up a strange, wild bay, or fjord, toward what appeared to be a little cluster of the plainest wood and stone huts imaginable, in a sheltered nook at the head of the fjord.

"That is Fiskenaes," said Roy, bobbing his head in the direction of the settlement. "It is a Danish trading-post. We are only a few miles farther north than we thought for. I shouldn't have come in here, however; but look at that ice!"

Scott looked behind them. The wind had evidently changed outside, for a great mass of huge icebergs and pack-ice and floe was following close upon their track.

"Just think if we were twenty miles farther back, or if we had not happened to be abreast this fjord when the ice struck in," said Roy.

The water about them was covered with kayaks and oomiaks now. There were Esquimaux, Danes and half-breeds, shouting a welcome to the strangers in words they could not understand, and evidently congratulating them upon having escaped the ice; while others upon the shore were waiting to welcome them when they landed.

The air grew foul with the vile odors of drying codfish, for Fiskenaes is the best place on all the coast for catching and drying cod. There was an exaggerated suggestion of home in that odor, and it might have

been rather agreeable to the boys had it not been saturated, through and through, with the viler smells of last year's whale fat, and seal and shark and walrus blubber, trying itself out into oil by natural processes, in great vats, in the open air.

They were glad enough, however, to find a temporary haven, and received a hearty welcome from the sturdy little Danish superintendent of the trading-post, who spoke English better than some Englishmen.

The *Snowbird* was warped into a sheltered cove, and in the afternoon the boys sat in the superintendent's office before a smoking oil-fire, watching the trades going on, as Esquimaux came from up and down the coast, and far in the interior, with their wives, all in their Sunday clothes with skins and furs and wal-

"WAITING TO WELCOME THEM."

rus ivory, frozen deer meat, cod, and all kinds of blubber, to exchange for tobacco and coffee.

"How in the world do they catch cod and seal in the interior?" Scott asked.

The superintendent smiled as he replied: "Greenland is full of fjords. Many of them you would hardly no-

A TRADER'S WIFE.

tice from the sea, but the fish find them, and the seal follow the fish for miles among the mountains."

"Are there any Esquimau villages in this neighborhood?" Roy asked.

" There are several small settlements that don't amount to much, but there's one quite extensive winter city a few miles inland, with summer quarters not far off upon a fjord. It will only require three days to go and come. I'll take you out there to-morrow, and you shall see the Esquimau in all his pristine glory," said the superintendent.

" Three days !" Scott exclaimed.

" To-morrow !" said Roy. " Why, we must try to get out of here this afternoon."

Again the superintendent smiled. " It will be more than three days, good friends, before you can escape us. That ice will not break up before a week."

They slept in the superintendent's house that night, in a room with solid wooden shutters to keep out the light, and when it was early morning by the clock they started for the Esquimaux.

Each one was armed, and each one carried a stock of provisions and

STARTING ON THE PICNIC.

seal-skin clothes upon his back, while a half-dozen dogs, loaded like so many miniature pack-mules, carried the tent and robes.

In the summer the ground was bare about Fiskenaes, and they were obliged to walk a little way to meet the sledges.

The superintendent added his little daughter to the pack upon his back. The boys thought she was a boy, for she was dressed in her Esquimau seal-skin clothes, which made her decidedly indignant, till her father explained to her how hard it was to tell men from women, when people first came to Greenland.

When they reached the sledges it was snowing, and they were all of them glad enough to put on the seal-skin clothes.

The rest of the burdens were securely packed upon the heaviest

sledge and started off, with six dogs and two Esquimaux harnessed in front and another pushing the sledge, while the fourth drove the dogs.

Two persons and a driver occupied each of the smaller sledges, and a moment later were flying like the wind over the white drifts.

The boys practiced with an instrument which the trader loaned them, to test their speed, on much the same principle of throwing the log at sea, and watched the driver handle his whip with unbounded admiration.

The dogs were attached to the sledge by long cords of rolled hide, of different lengths, and that whip was the only argument which the driver could use with them. The handle was only two feet long, but the lash was nearly eighteen feet.

When one dog lagged, or snapped at another, he called his name, in

STARTING THE BAGGAGE.

a shrill, sharp voice, shouted something like: " *Tu-lee-hec-hce-hee !* " and at the same instant lifted that short handle.

The lash was always dragging behind, but the driver gave a sudden jerk and it flew through the air.   The next instant there was a crack like the report of a pistol, and a yelp and a bound from the offending dog showed how correct the aim had been.

Scott borrowed the whip to try his hand.   No one at Little Harbor could crack a whip like him, and after a few experiments he could make a report that sent the Esquimau driver into ecstasies.

Then he watched for an offending dog, and had not long to wait. He gave an excellent imitation of " *Tu-lee-hec-hee-hee !* " and sent the lash flying; but it cracked upon the nose of the dog behind.   He yelped, fell back, stumbled and rolled over and over.   In the meantime the lash became entangled in the tow-lines.   The dogs discovered the fact in an

THE WINTER SETTLEMENT.

instant, and as that lash was the only thing they were afraid of, they stopped work forthwith, and began a grand free fight till everything was tangled.

It delayed them nearly half an hour, but fortunately there was no danger of approaching night to hasten them, and in time they reached the winter settlement. It was a cluster of hemispheres, made of cakes of ice, with a hole in one side for the people and dogs to creep in and out, and a hole near the top where the smoke could escape if it was in danger of dying for want of exercise.

The city was nearly deserted, as most of the families were at the fjord

THEY ENTERED THE LARGEST.

for the summer, and the boys crept into the largest hut. They were glad enough to get back into the open air again, however.

"Jehu!" said Scott, as he gulped a breath.

"Fiskenaes is bad enough," Roy gasped, coming out close behind him.

"It's only our regulation polar perfume," said the trader; "and that house has been unoccupied for some time. It must be pretty well aired out by this. You should try it in the winter, when three generations with a lot of untanned skins and blubber, live dogs and a whale oil fire

THE WALRUS HUNT.

get in there all together, and plug up the door and chimney hole in a cold snap. That's the real article."

"I should think the dogs would die, any way," Scott muttered.

"Die! why they like it. And so do the people. It is a very good thing for the traveling public, too. In the winter you could not distinguish one of these settlements at a little distance, and there are no roads or signboards, but you can smell an Esquimau village two or three miles away."

"I believe it," said Scott, as they took the sledges again and went on to the summer settlement at the head of the fjord, where the people were hunting and fishing, chattering like sea gulls round a wreck.

"The lazy fellows make their dogs do everything," Scott muttered, as they saw an Esquimau fix his harpoon in a large walrus basking on a piece of floating ice, and then leave his dog to land the creature by fastening the coil attached to the harpoon to the dog's harness.

"Just see those flowers!" Roy cried a moment later, as they came upon a cluster of bright native blossoms nestling on the southern side of

A SEAL-CATCHER.

a ledge of rocks, while ten feet away lay solid ice and snow.

"For the next month," said the trader, "wherever a bit of soil shows itself, they will make the most of it. Watercresses grow in a marsh behind my house; and around Julianshaab, at the south, a little grain grows in sheltered places, and coarse grass is a foot high, watered by the melting snow.   Fortunately, however, we don't eat what grows in the ground."

The boys looked at each other in astonishment.   It was something they had always known, but never stopped to appreciate.

" A whole nation," said Roy, " living without fruit or corn, wheat or

KOKO AND THE WOLVES.

vegetables, except as a few have learned and bought of foreigners !   But there's plenty of game, I suppose ? "

" In the winter a musk-ox sometimes finds himself driven down to us. I was out with a party last winter and took a huge fellow.   We have made two beds out of his hide.   That's his head up in the office.   Wolves are plenty, but they are more bother than they are worth.   Koko, tell them about the time you had with wolves last winter."

A sleepy Esquimau, sitting on the ice eating a piece of raw meat, grinned from ear to ear, and in broken English told how he left the settlement for the post with two barrels of fish oil on a sledge, when the wolves came at him.   Dogs will fight a white bear wherever they

SHOOTING THE MUSK-OX.

find him, but they will always run from a hungry wolf. The first thing the wolves killed one dog, and the rest all slunk away at the end of their ropes. Then the wolves came at him. He jumped into the largest barrel of oil, and with his harpoon kept the pack at a distance for a time. Then it occurred to him to upset the other barrel of oil, which he did, and while the wolves were going for that he started the dogs and left them.

"There are deer, too, but not many,' added the trader.

"And how about polar bears?" asked Roy. "I judged from pictures in my geography that they were floating on every iceberg, but I have not seen any."

"Strangers always think that way," said the trader, "but really white bears are very scarce. I never saw but three alive, but if the talk is true you may be fortunate. They tell me tracks have been seen around the camp for several days, and you might go and look them up to-morrow. If you can find the fellow we'll muster a crowd and go hunt him."

"I'll do it!" cried Scott.

"Me, too!" echoed

A SLEEPING BAG.

Roy; "and now let's turn in, so's to start as soon as possible."

"It is literally turn in," Scott exclaimed, as the sleeping arrangement was explained to him. "Look at this, will you, Roy? A sleeping bag, they call it. It's seven feet long, at least; that's good. All skin, with the fur inside, and this slit is the only opening. We must crawl into it feet first, and then, if it's a cold night, I suppose we pull the hole in after us. It's a nightgown and a half, I tell you."

Their beds were robes thrown on the snow, and they found the sleeping bags none too warm; while the trader told them of times when the mercury was 75 below freezing, when in his warmest clothing, covered with his sealskins, he had got bodily into the sleeping bag and pulled two heavy robes over that, and still found his feet frozen on waking.

With the pack-sled, a fresh lot of dogs and the best bear-hunter in the settlement, they started out to track the bear. They soon struck fresh prints in the soft snow. The driver stood up to obtain a better view. Things were very quickly becoming interesting. The dogs were rushing at a furious rate when, with a peculiar yelp, the whole pack made a sharp turn to the right, landing the driver on his head in a snowdrift.

Instantly the boys discovered a great, dingy-looking creature crouching in the snow ahead of them. He was much larger and not at all like the graceful, snow-white animal that rolls about in the Zoölogical Garden, but they knew that it must be the bear, and grasped their rifles.

Fortunately the sledge, unguided, struck an ice hummock and left both of the boys sitting in the snow; for a moment later the huge bear was crouching upon the sledge and snapping vigorously at the dogs.

Had they come near enough to his head he would have caught them in his teeth, given them one twist, and hurled them so far away that they would not care to come back again; but they had seen white bears before, and stood in a circle just out of reach, barking furiously, to take

THE BEAR CROUCHED UPON THE SLEDGE.

up his attention, while two behind him bit and bit and bit, whichever way he turned.

The hunter came running up from behind. They could not understand a word he said, but it was evident that he was anxious to have them follow him back to the settlement as quickly as possible.

" Well, I guess not!" said Scott.

" Not if we know ourselves," Roy added.

" Pray, Mr. Esquimau, what do you suppose we are here for?" Scott asked.

The poor fellow looked so earnest and bewildered that Roy took pity

ON THE SNOWBIRD'S DECK.

on him, shook his head, pointed to his gun, then at the bear, and motioned him to stand back and see the fun. The stupid fellow shook his head, but obeyed.

Presently the bear noticed them, deliberately turned about, and, with the dogs still hectoring him, came slowly toward them, snapping and snarling.

" Wonder what he eats?" Scott muttered, with a suggestive look down at himself.

" Not fruit or vegetables, any way," said Roy.

" Nor me, either, this morning," Scott added.

" How are you going to help it if he only bobs his head when you hit him, like your walrus, and comes right on ? "

" Do you s'pose he's bullet proof ? "

" We'll soon find out."

" What if he is ? "

" We'll have to run."

" Can't, in this snow."

" Let's try a shot. Are you ready ? "

" Aye! aye ! "

" You aim for his eye. That's soft, any way, and you're the best shot. I'll take him in the mouth, if he opens it. If not, I spot his nose! One ! "

UNLOADING STORES.

All the time the bear came nearer and nearer, his great claws glistening as he lifted them out of the snow.

" Two ! " The bear snarled, sat up on his haunches, threw his head back and showed a glistening row of teeth, precisely as though he were saying, " Come on, now. See if you can hurt me."

"Three!" Both rifles banged. The bear did not move except to close his eyes, shut his jaws with a resounding click, and draw his lips still farther back.

"Load again!" whispered Scott.

"Did we miss him?" Roy muttered.

"Not to-day!" Scott cried, as the bear began to sink slowly, and finally rolled over, dead, upon the snow.

He was given the place of honor on the sledge, while the boys walked and waded back to the settlement. He measured nearly nine feet, and

LANDING THE STORES.

weighed six hundred and eighty pounds as his body lay, the next day, stretched in triumph on the deck of the *Snowbird.*

During their absence the supply steamer from Denmark had come in, wedged her way into the outer ice, was made fast there with ice anchors, and such stores as were to be left at the post had been unloaded upon the ice. When the party returned the queer, sturdy, dumpy little Danish sailors were working the stores up to shore, with sledges and boats.

The captain had stopped at all of the ports of Greenland to the south, and the trader offered to find out if he knew anything of the *Louise.*

They were all sitting about the moss and oil fire in the office, waiting for the men to finish bringing up the stores, when they would begin the work of cutting the steamer out again.

Yes; he had seen the *Louise,* about three weeks before, and had

THE CAPTAIN ALMOST LEFT.

taken some freight from her hold for several of the Northern ports, as her captain was in haste to get away. She had loaded with saddle-back seal furs and oil, and had taken on about a dozen passengers for — for — for some port on the northern coast of Norway. He would think in a moment. But before he had thought there was a cry from the shore.

The ice was breaking up! He caught up his hood, pulled on his fur jumper and ran. The great iceberg on the outer edge had suddenly started out to sea, and the whole floe was following it. The steamer, of course, was set free, and must be got out of the dangerous position at once.

Two of the steamer's boats were still on the ice, nine of the sailors, and some of the stores.

The captain ran till he was met by a broad rift of open water, then yelled frantically for the men with one of the boats to come for him,

CHATTERING A FAREWELL.

while the people of the post rushed down to save the stores that were drifting away.

It was such a scene of confusion as Fiskenaes had never witnessed, and Scott and Roy, with the sailors of the *Snowbird* who were on shore, gave willing hands to help them out.

When the excitement was over, and they were getting the *Snowbird* into the fjord, it occurred to them that all they knew of the *Louise* was that three weeks before she had sailed for some northern port of Norway.

"Well, we're better off than if we knew nothing," said Roy. "I reckon there are precious few ports in Northern Norway, anyhow. The chart only gives five or six, and I move we run for the upper one as fast as wind will carry us, and then work down."

"I wish we had time to see more of Greenland," said Scott; "but I'm going to come again some day."

"Greenland is all pretty much alike, only in some places a little more so," said the trader. "A little colder north, a little warmer south. All you'd learn in twenty years would be to talk Esquimau, drink oil, and eat blubber and raw meat."

"I've read of wonderful old relics and ruins at the south," said Roy. "I should like to see them, but I'd rather be after the *Louise*." So they sailed away.

They were sorry to leave the hospitable superintendent at Fiskenaes, in spite of all the vile smells that surrounded him, and he was sorry to have them go. They even looked fondly back at the great waves dashing upon the base of a huge cliff jutting into the water, with the birds clinging to its ragged sides, chattering a farewell to them, and Puck, a handsome Spitz pup which the trader had given to Scott, barked in return.

"We shall be back here some day," said Roy, as he watched Cape Farewell sinking into the sea, and turning to the man at the helm, he set the course of the *Snowbird* toward Norway, the Land of the Midnight Sun.

CHAPTER VII.

THE LAND OF THE MIDNIGHT SUN.

DAY after day they held their course east by north; sometimes in sunshine, sometimes under clouds, always in broad daylight or a glowing sunrise and sunset.

With a great deal of pride they sighted the headlands of Iceland at the very day and hour they planned when off Cape Farewell, eight hundred miles away. They never dreamed that winds and tides and currents had been counteracting the deviation of their compass, and setting them right all by chance. It gave them too much confidence in their ability. They set the course again for Torghatten, about midway between the Naze and North Cape, some twelve hundred miles away, sure that they should hit it. But now the tides and currents and two sharp storms aided the deviations, and Arctic fogs prevented their taking the sun for seven full days.

They knew they had crossed the Arctic circle, for there was no perceptible change in the light through all the twenty-four hours. They were sure they had run over thirteen hundred miles, but a lookout had been kept at the masthead for two days before he reported: " Ship ahoy! A small steamer on the starboard bow!" and a half-hour later, " Land ahead! on the port bow."

They wondered at the absolute lack of vessels or any sign of life. The sun shone out clear and bright as they neared the defiant ledge, and they saw a dozen men pulling upon some sort of a cat-boat.

The *Snowbird* lay to, and Roy and Scott pulled ashore.

"Do any of you speak English?" Roy asked, and a curious shock it gave the boys when pretty much all of them replied with a chorus of, "Yes, sir!" "Oh! yes, indeed!" "Certainly!" and the like.

Roy was so taken by surprise that he forgot what he wanted to ask, and Scott put the question for him:

"What do you call this place?"

"North Cape, sir."

"North Cape!" Scott exclaimed.

"North Cape!" Roy gasped.

"We're seven hundred miles farther north than we thought for," said Scott in a low tone.

"We have sailed the *Snowbird* farther north than Europe or America, my boy," Roy returned triumphantly, striking a tragic attitude.

"LAND AHEAD!"

"But don't you ever let on how we came to do it, Roy," Scott added.

Among the men was a bright young Norwegian sailor who spoke excellent English, and knew the coast of Norway from cape to cape. He had been spending the season helping visitors to land and climb to the summit of the cape, but was anxious to get back to his home at **Chris-tiansand.**   He offered to pay his passage, but the boys contracted with him to act as their pilot instead.

Running to a hut he returned with his limited chest, and soon the *Snowbird* was under sail again ; for the boys cared nothing about the Midnight Sun, for which so many pilgrims make the journey and climb that precipitous ledge.

" I've seen quite enough of this twenty-four hours of daylight business," said Scott ; " and it's my humble opinion that when the proper time comes the sun ought to blow out his light and go to bed, and not be in any hurry about lighting up again too early in the morning, either."

Hammerfest was their first stopping-place. " It is the nearest city on earth to the North Pole," said the pilot, and the boys expected something w o r s e than little Fiskenaes. When they entered the fjord, however,

they found it literally crowded with shipping.   Quaint vessels of sturdy model lined the busy wharves.   Steep-roofed houses of ample dimensions stretched back as far as the eye could reach.   There were smoking fac-tories near the shore, and along the wharves were great store-houses, with open fronts, two stories up, for drying fish and skins, while church spires rose in the distance, and green grass and flowers appeared on the hillsides.

" Just think of it !" said Roy. " We're five or six hundred miles farther north than little Fiskenaes."

" They fish here every day of the year, and they have a great trade around North Cape with the northern part of Russia," said the pilot.

" Well, charity ought to begin at home," Scott replied. " We furnish

THE HEAD OF THE FJORD.

the hot water for the Gulf Stream that makes all the difference between this and Greenland, and then we go freeze to death ourselves, nearly two thousand miles south of here."

"It is quite true," said the pilot. "I am told that the winter at New England is often colder than at Hammerfest."

There was no *Louise* to be seen or heard from at Hammerfest, and after filling the water tanks, and stocking up with fresh fish and reindeer meat, they entered another fjord, long and winding, between rocky ledges, making their way toward Tromso.

"I suppose you do have ice and snow somewhere in these parts?" Scott observed.

"Most certainly!" exclaimed the pilot. "Tromso is so far back from the sea that it loses some of the effect, and there will be snow and ice now in the gorges. But Tromso even is still really only an island, though so far inland, and if you will give the time to working a little farther up

HAMMERFEST HARBOR.

the fjord and visit a Lapp settlement on the mainland, I'll show you snow and ice as old as any they've got in Greenland, and just as much of it."

"Well, I've seen snow and ice enough to keep me cool till next summer," said Scott. "But I'd like a peep at some Lapps, all the same."

"Me, too!" Roy exclaimed. "I have some very queer notions about

Lapps.   I don't know where I got them, but I'd like to see if they are
true."

So the *Snowbird* kept on and on, through passages so narrow that it
seemed almost impossible to pass, and over beautiful broad bays, always

UP THE FJORD TO TROMSO.

with a good sailing breeze, but
never with a single wave more
than a ripple, and bleak, bare, black mountains always rising precipi-
tately out of the water.

Half-way up the fjord they had an opportunity to take on board three
Lapps, and carry them to their destination.

They were a man and two women, the pilot said, but Scott declared
that until they were sorted out for him he could not for his life tell t'other
from which.

"They keep grinning like Esquimaux, but what squatty little things
they are!" Roy observed.   "See, this fellow doesn't come up to my
shoulder."

"They're as broad as they are long.   What makes them so big about
the waist?" Scott asked.

Here the Lapps all grinned again.   They could not understand Eng-
lish, but they saw there was some joke, and laughed, never dreaming it
was about themselves.

It was so ludicrous that the boys roared as the pilot explained that in

"WHERE YOU FIND MOSS YOU FIND REINDEER."

their primitive existence they had no Saratoga trunk or crocodile skin portmanteau, and when they were on the move, which was nearly all the time, they packed the contents of the pantry, the wardrobe, and all their household furniture in the bosoms of their loose blouse waists.

"Great Scott! Considering all the incidents, it strikes me those people must really be rather slim," Roy remarked, and the Lapps all laughed again.

Very soon they had an opportunity of seeing Lapps in abundance; some of them decided improvements upon the first samples. Some wore the *storhatten*, or "large hat," and some the *torghatten*, or "little hat,"

THE TROMSO CATHEDRAL.

which was really larger than the large hat. Aside from these, however, there seemed no system or fashion in their dress, but to get on as many pieces as they could.

"What perplexing work they must have dressing and undressing," said Roy.

"They do very little of that," replied the pilot, laughing scornfully, for the Norwegians all look down upon the Lapps. "They simply put on one piece after another as it grows colder, and take off one after another as summer comes on. They eat and work and sleep just as you see them."

"That's all right," said Scott. "What could you expect, Roy? Where Nature sets the example, by only one day and night a year, of course the people don't dress and undress but once. ''Twould be ag'in Natur,' as Aunt Sally used to say."

"THE LAPPS ALL GRINNED."

Clambering over rocks and moss they reached the valley where there was a summer settlement of Lapps, who followed the reindeer when they came down for six months of feeding on the moss.

"They live on reindeer," said the pilot. "They drink reindeer milk, eat reindeer meat, and wear reindeer skins. They make all their implements from reindeer bone and horn, and use the reindeer as their only means of traveling. The reindeer live on moss, so where you find moss you find reindeer, and where you find reindeer you find Lapps."

"I want a ride after a reindeer, if there is snow enough," said Scott.

"There's plenty of snow a mile from here," replied the pilot, "and if there were not, it would not matter, for they use the sledges on the bare ground just the same as on the snow." And while he went to make arrangements, the boys watched the daily operation of milking.

A Lapp would lasso the nearest doe and throw her down. Then some boy who was helping him would hold her by the great antlers till he had tied her feet, and he would proceed to milk.

"Jehu!" said Roy. "Isn't that just a straight tip for Aunt Sally and her frisky, one-horned cow? When we get home let's give it to her. It would save her and her milk-pail many a whack."

"I'll tell you what let's do," said Scott. "Let's go round and ask her if we can't show her on her one-horned cow, how they milk their kicking reindeer up in Lapland."

" Do you suppose she'd catch on ? " Roy asked thoughtfully.

" Well, no; but I reckon the cow would before we had done with her," Scott replied.

The pilot called them, having made the arrangements.   They walked a half-mile over some low hills.   There was snow enough in the next valley, and there were three reindeer harnessed like the dogs in Greenland, by a single cord, to three small sledges, looking almost like Indians' canoes.

" You don't expect us each to drive, do you ? " Scott asked, as he was told to seat himself in the first sledge and given the single rein and short-handed whip.   " I don't see how you steer with this one rope."

" There's little need to steer," replied the pilot.   " There are never but two places on a road in Norway.   One is the place you came from, the other is the place you are going to. All you have to do is to prevent a reindeer from

THE STORHATTEN.

stopping to eat, and he will go straight to the nearest settlement.   He can smell it, even if there is no road.   Only be sure you hold on to that rein when you upset, or the deer will go on without you."

" Well, I guess not," said Scott, and he took a double twist in the leather thong and caught it about his wrist.   It was a wise precaution, for both of the boys, as well as the pilot, capsized several times before they reached the village, nine miles away.

" Their houses are for all the world like the Esquimau huts," Roy exclaimed, " only these are made of mud and moss, and those were ice and snow."

THE TORGHATTEN.

Scott gathered courage to crawl into one, but Roy waited outside. " You ought to go in, Roy," he gasped, as he emerged again.   " It's a fine place; twice the size of a Greenland mansion, and on top of all the other smells they've carpeted and bedded the thing with undressed skins."

" I've had fun enough out here, killing mosquitoes," said Roy. " The place is thick with them. Let's get out. And by the way, did you see that fellow in snowshoes ten feet long, as we came up, with a back full of ducks and a long pole with a slicer on the end of it ? "

" They were ice-shoes, not snowshoes," said the pilot. " With them he can follow duck over ice not more than a quarter of an inch thick. But they are best of all for coming down hill. He climbs all day up and up after game, then he puts on those shoes, and guiding himself with that slicer, will come down the mountains twenty miles an hour."

" Well, I didn't see him at all," said Scott, "for looking at the baby. You know the woman who stood smoking a pipe and talking with him ?

THE LAPPS AT HOME.

I tell you she knew a thing or two. But the baby! Jehu! the baby! Did you ever see a baby like that in all your life ? "

" Never saw a baby at all but you, Scott, and I was too young then to appreciate the privilege."

" Come off, Roy !" cried Scott, laughing. " Didn't I rock the cradle and keep the flies off you, so that you could go right on teething without tacking ? "

" I wish you would practice a little now, and keep these mosquitoes off," said Roy.

On their return they were offered the cordial and dirty hospitality of the Lapps, in the shape of a greasy bowl of warm reindeer milk. Roy tried, but could not get the bowl to his lips. Scott profited by the hint, and caught up a spoon made of reindeer horn.

" A real horn spoon," he muttered, wiping off a quantity of grease from the edge with an old piece of newspaper from his pocket, but one swallow was enough.

" It's fine and sweet," he said, "but either from its surroundings or from what those creatures eat, it carries with it a strong impression of tired codfish."

Their last view of the Lapps was a smiling mother, shaking her baby to sleep in a portable cradle.

A little later the *Snowbird* was working her way through the circuitous

"THAT FELLOW IN SNOWSHOES."

fjords off the Loffoden Islands, a short sail to the south. They are as much a part of Norway as Norway herself; only great, ragged, precipitous mountains cut entirely away from each other by those beautiful black arms of waveless water. They were bound for the little town of Svolvaer, located there simply because people had found a little strip of earth large enough to build upon. It was only another possible port for the *Louise*, and they proposed to test them all.

The pilot was in charge. Roy was watching the cliffs, and Scott, with Puck beside him keeping a sharp lookout, was indulging in his old trade of fishing.

He had had excellent luck, when it suddenly occurred to him that the *Snowbird* was running within twenty feet of those bristling ledges, and he began to wonder if it was safe.

"Do you know how much water we have under us?" he called to the pilot. The pilot shook his head.

"Hadn't we better take soundings?" Scott asked as Roy came up.

"I think we had, or else slack up a bit," said Roy; for they were spinning along before a rousing breeze.

A PORTABLE CRADLE.

They threw the lead. They threw it twice. One hundred fathoms of line went out. It was all the line there was, but it did not touch bottom.

"There's nearer twice that, sir," said the pilot, a little hurt that they had doubted his ability.

"How in the world is that possible?" Roy exclaimed, looking at the ledge rising out of the water so near to them.

The pilot shrugged his shoulders and simply answered:

"This is Norway, sir."

"I knew 'twas the Land of the Midnight Sun," said Scott, "but it strikes me it's all sun and bare rocks, with no land and no bottom."

" I'll tell you how Norway came to be," said the pilot, "and you shall judge for yourself."

" It was this way," said the pilot, as they were running southward. " When God created the world, he looked at it, saw that it was good, and

SVOLVAER ON THE LOFFODENS.

rested. While he slept Satan came out to look. It was too beautiful for him, and he tore a great rock from the bed of hell and threw it at the earth. It fell near the North Pole, flattening down the perfect sphere, shaking the pole out of the perpendicular, and splitting into a thousand pieces. God woke and put his hand upon the earth and kept it from tipping any farther. He scraped up from the Sahara a little soil. It wasn't much, but he threw it over the bare black rocks. You will still find it down in the valleys. That is why the axis of the earth is not perpendicular; why the earth is flattened at the pole; why the Sahara is nothing but sand, and why Norway is. Poor Norway! God has sent her fish in recompense. It was all he could do."

The pilot really sighed, and Scott and Roy learned afterward that he had told them a legend actually accepted by many as the only way of accounting for such a place as Norway.

SCOTT AND LUCK FISHING.

"That is Torghatten on the port bow, sir," said the pilot. "It is named 'little hat,' after the things the Lapps wore, you remember. See how much it is like them? Soon we shall be round on the other side, and you will see a hole completely through the mountain, like a tunnel. Long ago, you know, there were giants in Norway, and one, Hestmand, fell in love with Lekö. She would not have him, and on horseback he chased her. She had a brother who was a giant. He picked her up and carried her out into the sea. Hestmand rode out into the water a few

"THAT'S TORGHATTEN."

miles below. When the brother was so far out that only his torghatten showed above the water, Hestmand fired an arrow at him. It went right through his hat. One of the gods was looking on. He didn't like Lekö for running away from a man who loved her. He didn't like her brother for helping her. He didn't like Hestmand for firing at them, so he turned the whole of them to stone, just where they were."

"Where is Hestmand?" asked Scott.

"Just below, sir. You'll soon see how like a man on horseback it looks, to this day."

"And you believe it all?" Roy asked in astonishment.

"Why not, sir?" replied the pilot solemnly. "If I doubted it I could climb right up and walk through that hole in Torghatten to convince myself." But there was a peculiar twinkle in his eye as he walked away.

It was by no means difficult navigating. They could have managed without a pilot, by careful watching, but, as Scott expressed it: "It is an inexpressible convenience to have some one on board to answer questions," and Roy put his sentiment more characteristically for him: "It is no end of relief to feel that there's some one to take off the edge of responsibility."

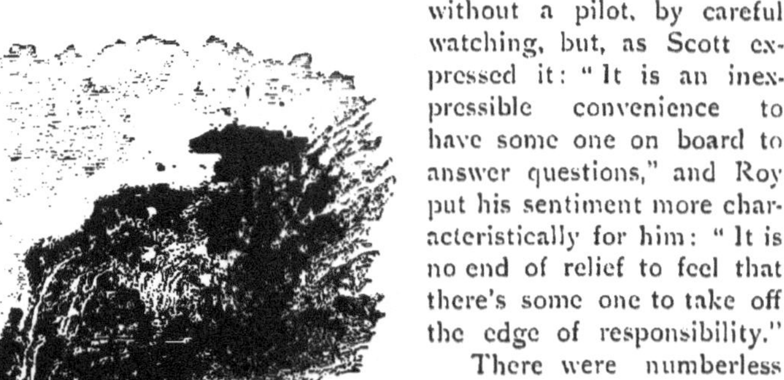

There were numberless islands, but always the deepest of deep water between them, and it was only when running up the fjords that the pilot stood constantly at the prow to point out the way.

"With this soft air and all, it would be hard to realize that we were still north of the Arctic Circle," said Roy, "if it were not for the sun. I'm thinking that after this lot of extra daylight we've had we shall hardly know how to manage in the dark."

"Well, I'm thinking," Scott replied, "that I'd like to square up the account by seeing this coast during the night. It didn't seem so out of place in Greenland. I could as easily imagine those fellows enveloped in a six months' night as I could a blueberry bear going into a hollow tree for the winter. They're a stupid, sleepy set, any way, and I fancy they enjoy it. But think of a busy town like Hammerfest with no sunlight; I can't."

"I never thought of it that way," said Roy, "but it is funny, isn't it? I wonder how they manage."

"They must sail by chronometer, of course," Scott replied; "but I tell you what it is, these twenty-four hour clocks would be a great game in this climate, wouldn't they? I should think they'd be in danger of getting all twisted up and coming out in the spring counting the wrong twelve hours for day."

"Precious little harm it would do, Scott," said Roy; "for after they got over the first spasm of changing it would be daylight all the time, and they could keep right on with it just as before."

"The principal change they make is in their homes," the pilot re-

TORGHATTEN FROM THE BAY.

marked. "The houses usually face east and west, and are often divided by a straight hall, with a whole house on each side. Many families who can afford it live entirely upon the south side of the house during the winter, and upon the north side during the summer months."

Thus with clear weather and a fair wind they ran southward till they crossed the Arctic Circle. over seas so smooth that one could hardly believe them a part of the thundering ocean, and were headed for the fjord of Trondhjem.

CHAPTER VIII.

ROY and Scott turned in, leaving the pilot to work the *Snowbird* up the long fjord of Trondhjem. Roy was asleep almost as soon as he touched the bunk; for while there could be no waves to rock the sailor boy's cradle, there was a strong breeze blowing in a fog, which kept the *Snowbird* in constant motion.

Scott was almost asleep, too, when he heard the pilot call:

"Captain Sargent!"

"Aye, aye!" Scott replied, seeing that Roy did not answer.

"There's a two-master, square-rigged, American-built brig, mainsails and jib set, two miles from the offing on the starboard bow, sir."

Scott leaped from his bunk, up the companion-way, grasped the pilot's glass, and was looking at the point indicated, in the twinkling of an eye.

He was none too soon, for the fog was rapidly closing in, and in a moment she was lost to sight. The effect of that momentary glimpse, however, was remarkable. Scott sprang to the helm, and noted on the compass the point where the brig had disappeared. He caught the helm, put the *Snowbird's* beak in that direction, ordered the sailor whose place he had taken to go below and call the captain, telling him to dress and come on deck; then, turning to the pilot, said:

"Go forward and keep a sharp lookout. Mind you don't let me waste time in turning out too far for rocks. I'm going to overhaul that craft if it takes the *Snowbird's* keel."

Two more sailors were called to work the sails, and when Roy came up the companion-way, had he not been impressed with the fact that something of grave importance had occurred, he would surely have burst into an uproarious laugh. There stood Scott at the helm, with every

HESTMAND.

nerve and muscle strained, his long brown hair that had not seen a barber for three months at least, drifting where it would, his bare feet firmly planted on the cold, wet deck, his teeth set, and his nightgown whipping about him in the wind like a torn sail. Regardless of everything, he was keeping the *Snowbird* bowling along as close to the wind as he could, hold her.

Scott simply said, "*Louise!*" and motioned forward with his hand. Roy made for the prow. But it was starboard and port; it was twist and turn, in and out among rocks and islands, through the heavy, drifting fog, till they were almost back again to Hestmand, and after twelve hours of dodging, tacking, careening, bumping more than once and straining their eyes in vain, they gave up in despair and headed again for the Trondhjem fjord.

"That was the *Louise*, or I'm an Esquimau!" Scott muttered.

"Well, she'd not be round here now. any way," Roy replied.

"She was going south when I called you, sir," said the pilot.

"She was headed due west when I saw her," Scott added.

"From which she was just as likely to be going northeast in reality, as any other way," Roy put in; "for a snake wouldn't twist any more than we have to, to get around these rocks."

"I think she was either going in or coming out from Trondhjem, sir," said the pilot.

"That's explicit," Scott growled, for he was not at all satisfied with their night's work. "It means that either we shall find her or we sha'n't. I like to work on a sure thing, like that."

"Well, it's all that's left us," said Roy. "And it's a good deal to know that she's in these waters. If she's been in here we shall hear from her. If she's waiting for the fog to lift she'll follow us. If she's gone in already we shall find her. You've caught cold, Scott, running through the fog in your

THE FORTRESS OF MONKHOLMON.

nightgown. Take some quinine and a good sleep, and I'll stay on deck. If we sight the northeast shadow of her ghost, I'll call you."

Scott was not called. They entered the fjord, passing the little fortress of Monkholmon, and for the first time ran the little *Snowbird* under the cannon's mouth. It was a very quiet cannon, however, and so was the famous fjord up which they wound their way.

Here and there they passed

STOREHOUSES OF TRONDHJEM.

enormous storehouses, where fish were drying and dried, and through a rift in the hills they could occasionally catch glimpses of the spires and towers of Trondhjem's cathedral, while the pilot repeated some of the

IN THE CATHEDRAL PORCH.

grand old stories of Norwegian lore; of King Olaf who founded Trondhjem almost a thousand years ago; how his mother fled with him from Norway, when he was a baby prince, to save his life from a usurper; how he was captured by pirates, sold as a slave, escaped, married an Irish maid, was converted to her religion, returned to Norway, became king and at once christianized the whole of Norway at the point of the sword.

Another turn in the fjord brought the city of Trondhjem into full view as it lay upon a low hill, completely surrounded by the great mountains of Norway.

"It was in yonder cathedral," said the pilot, "that our good King Oscar II., and his queen Sophia, were crowned, in the summer of 1873."

TRONDHJEM.

The *Snowbird* dropped anchor where she could quickly be got under way, in case the *Louise* appeared. The pilot was to keep a lookout and run up a signal in case she was seen, while the boys took the gig and went on shore to learn what they could from the wharves.

Everything seemed solemn and still. Nothing was going on any where; but they were assured that no brig named *Louise*, no vessel at all from America, had been in port there for months.

They must wait at least a day to see if she was coming; and to make the best of it they wandered about the quaint and quiet old city.

They climbed the hill to the cathedral, fantastically decorated with men and animals in every conceivable shape and size. Cautiously they entered the open door, where several women in bright and very pretty costumes sat in a sort of vestibule, with two or three uneasy children.

"I'll bet it's a christening!" Roy whispered. "They're waiting out here till the sermon's done."

"Sermon!" Scott muttered with a short gasp. "It is Sunday, isn't it? and that is why everything's so still?"

"I believe it must be, Scott. I say, we haven't had much opportunity for preaching lately. Let's go in."

They pulled off their hats, and very gravely and solemnly crept through the open door. They were more thoroughly frightened than when they faced the polar bear or knew that the *Snowbird* was sailing directly over the famous Maelstrom, south of the Loffoden Islands.

They seated themselves on the very first bench they could reach, and sat with folded hands, reverently looking up at the tall man in a long black gown and a great white ruff, who was standing in a high pulpit evidently preaching a sermon. In their embarrassment they sat in this way for nearly ten minutes before they realized that he was preaching in Norwegian, and they could not understand a word he said.

In time they became uneasy, and nudging Roy with his foot, Scott whispered:

"Let's cast off. Do you suppose there's any law against going out?"

THE TRONDHJEM CATHEDRAL.

"What's the matter with staying? We don't get any too much church nowadays," Roy whispered back.

"I know it," said Scott, "but I can't help it. I'll be asleep in one minute more."

Roy looked cautiously over his shoulder, and seeing a clear coast, crept quickly and silently out again, followed by Scott.

"WHERE IT IS NOT UPHILL, IN NORWAY, IT IS SURE TO BE DOWNHILL."

The *Snowbird* lay below without a signal, so they went on over the hill, past pretty little cottages and queer-looking peasants in thick wooden shoes, pausing to examine several specimens of ancient Norwegian architecture, and coming to a full stop before a vehicle at which they stared in blank astonishment.

There were two wheels and two strong thills. They protruded behind the axle, where they were united by a curved arm, and they evidently protruded in front of the horse when he was harnessed into them. Between the horse and axle a curious contrivance rose above the thills, very much like the bowl of a spoon, forming a seat just large enough for one. There was no floor under it, but two large iron loops attached to the thills seemed intended for footrests.

"What a funny contrivance," said Roy, with a laugh.

"Wonder if that fair-faced fossil standing beside it belongs to it," Scott remarked.

"He wouldn't know enough to tell you if you asked him," Roy replied. "It's a Norwegian sulky of ancient date, I reckon. Let's go on."

"Wait till you see me scrape acquaintance with him, through the great volapuk of signs," said Scott, stepping toward the man.

He paused for a moment, with his hands in his pockets, wondering how to begin, when

IN THE PULPIT.

the fellow turned half-about, and with a pleasant smile remarked:

"That, gentlemen, is a carjol " (he pronounced it car-y-ole), " the only native carriage of Norway. It holds but one, beside a possible driver seated there behind, for where it is not downhill in Norway, it is sure to be uphill, and our little ponies have all they can do to manage one passenger apiece. I worked in a mill at Hartford, on the Connecticut River, for ten years, and saw a good deal of your country. If you will accept my carjols and ponies for an hour or two I should like to show you some of mine."

Without waiting for a reply, which it might have been embarrassing to prepare, he trudged leisurely away and soon appeared leading two stubbed little ponies which he harnessed into two carjols.

Each boy had to drive for himself, while the host seated himself behind the first carjol, where he could walk up and down the steepest hills and converse with both the boys. Huge rocks, and mountains bleak and bare and black swept up in great precipitous ledges. Waterfalls were everywhere; rising in the clouds and plunging down, varnishing the rocks with purple as they passed — leaping, roaring, thundering till in clouds of spray and tangled rainbows they plunged into some dark fjord down below.

Such was the glimpse of Norway which Roy and Scott obtained in a drive of two hours, bumping along in the only wheeled vehicle which can accommodate itself to that grand and wonderful country.

They stopped to rest and lunch with a friend of their host, living upon another fjord. He could not speak a word of English, but the boys were astonished to find that they understood a good deal of what he said.

NORWEGIAN PEASANT.

"Why," said the miller, "before I could speak any English I was in the Scotch Highlands, and could easily understand the peasants there, and they could understand me; but in London I could not understand a thing. Now it is quite changed since I have learned English. I can understand Englishmen, but can make nothing out of the Scotch dialect."

On their return they saw a fellow sitting alone upon a green bank, so engrossed in playing a violin that he did not look up as they passed.

A GLIMPSE OF NORWAY.

" You have fiddles here, at any rate," said Scott.

" Fiddles?" replied the miller. " Have you forgotten that this was the home of Ole Bull?"

The first glimpse of the *Snowbird's* mast showed them that the *Louise* had not appeared. They arranged with the miller to telegraph them at Bergen if she came in and sailed away to that ancient little city, brimming full of rare old stories of Norwegian lore of the days when the Vikings roamed the sea, and when the kings of Norway were crowned at Bergen; but it had not a word for them of the *Louise*,

"WHAT A FUNNY CONTRIVANCE."

and again they arranged to be notified at Christiansand, the most southern city of Norway, and the little *Snowbird* rounded the Naze, and among beautiful islands, huge rocks and wild mountain fjords, came out upon the broad, smooth bay which lies before Christiansand; one of the most picturesque and tempting resting places to be found in the wide, wide world.

Their only glimpse of the city, however, was that one view from the bay; for as soon as the *Snowbird* appeared a boat put out from the shore to meet her, with a telegram for Captain Royal Sargent, American bark *Snowbird*, from the port of Bergen:

" The brig *Louise* is anchored here."

Even before the *Snowbird* lost her headway she was put about. A double watch was kept all the way back, but in the dozen different passages among the islands there was every chance to pass within a mile or two and never see her. At Bergen a message from the miller awaited them:

" The brig *Louise* is at the wharf."

They sailed again to that distant fjord, only to find that she had loaded for Christiania, and sailed a week before.

"Captain Downing has gone mad!" said Roy decidedly; but they sailed back again over the same path — half of the entire length of Norway, for the third time, to Christiansand, and almost as much farther up the Skager-Rack and Christianian fjord to the modern capital of Norway. At first they thought of going across Norway, by almost the only railroad in the country, from Trondhjem to Christiania, but decided on the chances of overtaking the *Louise*, and crowding on all the sail which the *Snowbird* could carry they urged her on till the summer palace of the king appeared before them overlooking the fjord from a beautiful knoll, rising above the capital.

There was little about this city that was suggestive of the wild, grand country to which it belonged. They walked for an hour down the broad clean streets, bordered with low, substantial, tile-roofed houses. They paused for a moment before the stern and solid Parliament buildings, but

NATURE ABOUT TRONDHJEM.

it was simply while they waited, nervously enough, for the water-tanks to be filled, and a fresh stock of provisions to be taken on board; for, to their utter chagrin, they heard only the same old story: the *Louise* had been there, and only four-and-twenty hours before had sailed for Stockholm, the capital of Sweden.

"THE HOME OF OLE BULL."

"Roy Sargent!" Scott exclaimed, "I wish you'd kick me from here to North Cape and back again, overland all the way. It would do me good. It took us two months to reach Trondhjem from home, and before we see Stockholm we shall have thrown away almost two months

BERGEN.

more knocking up and down this coast. Why in the world didn't I agree with you to come here by rail?"

"I thought just as you did," Roy replied. "And I'll kick you up to North Cape if you'll kick me back here again. But we'd better put it off, just now, and make for Stockholm."

Changing pilots, as their Norwegian friend was not acquainted with the coast beyond, they sailed up the Cattegat, only catching a glimpse, here and there, of the coast towns of Sweden; enough to realize that in surrounding foliage, as well as mountains and architecture, they were very different from treeless, rocky Norway, and at last, with winter close upon them, entered the great harbor of Stockholm.

Two pairs of sharp eyes bent to one end, were not long in penetrating the forest of masts lying along the wharves, and discovering the familiar outline of the brig *Louise*, upon whose deck they had been cleaning cod-fish in the early springtime, a few months before, little dreaming of what lay in the near future.

The *Snowbird* came to anchor in the bay, and with pale faces and trembling hands Roy and Scott pulled away in the gig, straight for where the *Louise* was lying.

What did they care for the great city, that beautiful Venice of the North, with all its canals, its huge steamers, its great ships from all over the world, its royal palace rising above the city like some monster coming up out of the sea, its great warehouses, its tall and graceful church spires, its statues and monuments everywhere, its long line of

"CHRISTIANSAND, A TEMPTING RESTING PLACE."

fisher women coming down the wharf? Their eyes and thoughts were bent upon the brig *Louise*.

Flags of all nations were flying about them, but they did not even notice that the red, yellow and blue of Sweden floated from the masthead of the brig. They were watching her deck, and, making the gig fast, they gained that point without delay.

A Swedish sailor sat smoking upon a coil of rope. He answered Scott's inquiry for Captain Downing with a shrug of his shoulders, a shake of his head and a long-drawn " Y-a-a-s."

" Is he on board?" said Roy.

CHRISTIANSAND.

" Y-a-a-s," replied the sailor.

" Tell him that we want to see him at once," said Scott.

" Y-a-a-s," drawled the sailor, with a pleasant grin, still solemnly shaking his head.

" Well, why don't you start?" Roy exclaimed, impatiently stamping his foot.

Seeing that something must be done, the sailor withdrew his pipe, shrugged his shoulders again, grinned from ear to ear, and still shaking his head, remarked apologetically:

" Me no sabe, sir, me no sabe."

STREET OF CHRISTIANIA.

THE SUMMER PALACE, CHRISTIANIA.

" Well, is there any one on board who does?" Roy cried, while Scott, too impatient to stand still longer, started for the cabin by the path he knew so well.

As he reached the foot of the companion-way, he discovered a burly, red-nosed, weather-beaten fellow, sprawled out there at his ease, smoking a huge pipe and drinking from an enormous mug of beer.

" I want to see the captain," Scott began without ceremony.

" Y-a-a-s," replied the stalwart seaman, without lifting his eyes.

"Well, I want to see him now," said Scott.

"Y-a-a-s," replied the giant, taking a leisurely whiff from his pipe.

Very slowly, very loud, and somewhat savagely from his curbed excitement, Scott repeated:

"I want to see the captain of this brig *Louise.*"

"Y-a-a-s," drawled the other, watching the smoke as it curled away.

Fortunately, Roy appeared at this moment, and Scott turned to him in utter disgust.

"I say, Roy, here's another of these 'no sabe' chaps, making himself at home as though he belonged here, and agreeing with everything I say."

"What in the name of wonder is Captain Downing doing with such a crowd?" Roy replied, and turning to the big fellow he tried his hand, shouting in his plainest English:

"The captain! captain! Want to see the captain! Come, Dutchie, you can surely understand that much."

Very slowly the fellow took his pipe from his mouth, lifted his sleepy

PARLIAMENT HOUSE, CHRISTIANIA.

eyes till they rested upon the two excited boys, and very deliberately he replied:

"O, y-a-a-s! I onderstant dot mouch blenty vell py dis dime. No

STOCKHOLM.

need to spile your voice. Five dimes you dells me you vants de captain
of dis prig *Louise*, and five dimes I dells you y-a-a-s, I. vas at your
service.   Ven you don't got satisfied mit dot, I dells you y-a-a-s again."

" Are you the captain of this brig *Louise?*" Scott gasped.

The fellow brought his big fist down on the table, exclaiming:

A GLIMPSE OF SWEDEN.

" Mein Gott! I give it to
you shoust vonce more: y-a-a-s!
Now s'pose you got any pees-
ness; better drop dot mouch
und sbeak him oud, ain't it ? "

Scott and Roy looked at each other for a moment in utter bewilder-
ment, and Roy was actually upon the point of repeating that same old
question, when the fellow pushed back his mug of beer, laid down his
pipe and, with a facial contortion which was evidently intended for a
genial smile, remarked :

" Kome, now, young fellars, vat you vants mit de captain of dis prig
Louise?"

" We don't want anything of you," said Scott. " We want Captain
Downing."

" Vell, you komes good vays afterwards for dot," he replied slowly,
drumming on the table. " Dree monds ago I sinks my sheep in a pig

storm, py St. John's, Newfoundlant, und me und mine sailors is shoust vaiting dere for somedings, ven oup komes dis Captain Downing und de prig *Louise.* Vell, he vants to seel, und I vants to puy. So."

"Well, where is he and his daughter now?" Roy asked.

"Vere's a flee vat pites me last somer?" he replied with a hoarse laugh. "I done know. He sheats me like everydings on dis prig, und he don't sheat me no more, nor no odder Yankee."

"Can't you tell us which way he went?" Scott asked.

"O, y-a-a-s!" he drawled, returning to his pipe. "He dakes dot

"FISHER WOMEN COMING DOWN THE WHARF."

gall, und goes on poard a sdeamer pound for Denmarks, mit my plessing und my monish; y-a-a-s."

Scott and Roy returned to the *Snowbird* and set her beak across the water westward, over the Baltic Sea and into the Gulf of Finland.

Their last glimpse of Stockholm was a merry crowd of fisherwomen, barefooted, or in thick wooden shoes, coming singing down the wharves, with their day's catch in baskets made of coarse grass.

"I'll tell you, Roy, Captain Downing has got a head on him," said Scott. "He was too big a man for codfishing. Here he has been in Russia for three full months at least, while we have been waltzing through the Arctics after the shadow of his old reefer."

"I wonder what he's been doing with himself," said Roy. "He must have got pretty well settled by this time. I thought all the time that he was mad, but I guess you were right. Who'd have thought of his selling the *Louise* and making a short cut, that way."

"I reckon fact's stranger than fiction, every time," Scott replied. "And when you're done,

if we get him in the end, and it all comes out right, I'm not sorry that even a fool's errand took us through the Arctics."

"Nor I!" said Roy, decidedly.

CHAPTER IX.

THE *Snowbird* entered the Gulf of Finland, bounding on with a northwest wind that was sharp and keen like Greenland. Winter was coming down upon them in earnest.

At mid-day it was still warm, however, and then the fishing smacks were still abundant, dodging about, pointed at stem and stern alike.

One, that shot close under the stern of the *Snowbird*, made Scott's heart beat fast and his cheeks grow red, all because beside the angular old fisherman holding his craft to the wind, sat his daughter, with flaxen hair and clear blue eyes, and a sober, earnest face. She was so much like Vera — more like Vera than any one he had ever seen before; yes, Vera, too, was a Russian. It was only the great family resemblance of nations, no doubt, and Scott, ashamed of himself, tried to remember that all that he was doing, trying to do, and determined to do, was to the end that Vera should go back to Russia and be beyond all thought of him forever, and still his heart beat fast in spite of him, all because a girl who reminded him of Vera, in a rude fishing smack, shot under the lee of the *Snowbird*.

"Just look at that village up the river yonder," Roy exclaimed.

"Bother the village!" Scott replied. "I want St. Petersburg."

It was not much of a village; only a half-dozen fantastic houses, a few fantastic people, two windmills for grain and lumber, and a wonderfully fantastic church. It was a real little exponent of Russia, however,

"JUST LOOK AT THAT VILLAGE."

just as Fiskenaes was of Greenland, St. John's of Newfoundland, Trondh-
jem of Norway; just as the fisherman's daughter was like Vera, because
they were both Russians — the little village was very like its country.

The *Snowbird* flew onward till met by a harbor police-boat, and an
officer who ordered them to drop anchor off Kronstadt, at the entrance
to the bay of Peterhof, twenty miles below St. Petersburg, and right

"SHE WAS SO MUCH LIKE VERA."

under the mouth of a dozen yawning cannon, in the little round forts
protecting the entrance.

The official could speak French, but no English, and the pilot acted
as interpreter.

A strange feeling of dread crept over the boys. A ponderous official
in a gorgeous uniform, had deliberately taken command of their little
Snowbird, and now he proceeded to take command of them.

He demanded their papers.

Papers?   They had none.   Then their commissions?   They never had any.   Their passports?   They had never obtained any.   Had they anything, reasonable or unreasonable, to justify their coming deliberately into the harbor of Kronstadt?

"We own the *Snowbird*, for the time being, at least.   We carry no passengers.   We carry no freight.   We ask no favors of any one," Scott declared.

"Precisely," replied the official; "which makes it the more incumbent upon me to ask what you are here for."

"On business," Roy replied.

"Evidently," said the official, with an insinuating smile.   "Will you tell me what business?   It will be quite necessary before you advance."

UNDER THE GUNS OF KRONSTADT.

"I don't think I hardly could," Roy responded, looking at Scott. "Then I shall be obliged to find out for myself," said the official. At which Scott's nature, which many a time had got the better of his

ALEXANDER'S COLUMN

judgment, sprang to the front, and with his hands well down in his
pockets, and his head a little on one side he replied:

"I'll bet this bark that you don't find out what our business is unless
we decide to tell you."

The officer made no reply, but quietly invited the boys to enter his
steam launch.

They realized that it was really a command, and with the strong

THE BRIDGE OVER THE NEVA.

argument of a dozen well-armed marines just below, and half of the
cannon of Kronstadt within range, they decided to accept.

They were placed in comfortable quarters, but kept constantly under
guard.

At the end of three days they were brought before a magistrate, and
told their story. Then for a week more they were kept in close con-
finement, unable to obtain one word of information about anything.

A change came, however. They were taken on board a police-boat,
sent down into a dingy cabin where they could see nothing but water,
and carried for twenty miles up the bay. Then they were taken on shore.

A magnificent city burst suddenly upon their view as they emerged from the dark cabin. The police-boat lay on the bosom of a broad river. High walls of rose-granite on either side, held it within bounds. They knew that it must be the Neva. A massive stone bridge was before

STATUE OF THE TZAR NICHOLAS.

them. Broad avenues extended in different directions, and massive buildings rose on every hand.

One glimpse of St. Petersburg ! then they were hurried into a carriage that was evidently waiting for them. With a coachman and footman in livery, and with mounted soldiers in front and behind, they started at a breakneck pace, through the broad streets of Russia's capital.

"I call this rather fine in its way," said Scott, leaning back in the upholstered carriage. " How old-fashioned everybody looks ! "

"I believe they run on the old calendar in Russia, with Christmas and New Year's twelve days behind ours, and perhaps they have never caught up in anything else either," said Roy.

" Do you suppose that we are prisoners, Roy ? "

" Looks like it, doesn't it ?   I never was a prisoner before, and I don't know how it feels, but I rather guess that we are prisoners of the Tzar."

" I don't mind it much, do you ? " said Scott.

" I'd rather be in open water on the deck of the *Snowbird*."

" I wouldn't, until I'd seen St. Petersburg ; and as far as the coach goes this isn't a bad way to see it, for a change. Look there, now, isn't that a fine old arch? See those bronze horses. Do you suppose real horses ever pranced like that? Glory! how we spun under it ! "

" Jehu ! " Roy exclaimed, as they drew near a great square, with a graceful pillar, one round shaft of highly polished rose-granite, eighty feet high, upon an enormous pedestal, towering nearly thirty feet in the air. " I wish they'd drive slower, for with no chart of the city, and no pilot aboard, a fellow wants to have a good long look at things to remember them and find out afterwards what they are."

" Bother what they are ! " said Scott, laughing. " They're every bit as fine to me as though I knew a dozen names for them. Look at that statue, now, and — oh ! just look at the pedestal. Whew! that was fine. I suppose it was some Tzar, or saint, or something or other ; but what difference does it make ? "

" I do wish he'd drive slower," Roy repeated, as they turned swiftly round another corner, changing the scene entirely to a series of public buildings of some sort, decorated with massive columns on every hand, and statues everywhere, with a beautiful garden upon their right.

" Do you mind the style of the one-horse teams, Roy ? For all the world they're like pictures I've seen of Irish jaunting-cars, only they are lower, and have four wheels instead of two."

" Didn't have time to notice the vehicles," Roy replied. " I was look-ing at the drivers' hats and at those big loops from the ends of the thills going over the horses' heads. I wonder what earthly use they are ! "

" If everything you see has got to have its use explained to you, you'd best ask the Government to send a guide along, next time it transfers us," Scott answered, laughing heartily. " The fact is, I don't care a straw whether a statue is used to hold down a pedestal, or the pedestal to hold up the statue."   .   .

" At any rate, I'll bet that the next time you come to Russia you'll bring your business card with you, and present it before it is called for," said Roy.

" P'r'aps I shall and p'r'aps I sha'n't," said Scott, reflecting for a moment. " I'll tell you what it is, Roy ; I reckon that Russia is a pretty tough place to get into successfully, and I shouldn't wonder if, in the end, we found that we had got into it just as successfully, if not quite so gracefully, as if we had worked it all up in advance."

" I wish I had your hopeful heart, Scott. It's a grand thing when one gets into trouble."

" Well, I wish I had your level head, Roy. It's a regular field-marshal for keeping one out of trouble."

Here their carriage dashed toward an enormous building, stretching

" THEY TURNED ANOTHER CORNER."

for nearly a quarter of a mile upon the broad street and as far back upon a side street. It was three stories high, magnificently decorated, and guarded at every entrance by armed soldiers, while over the principal entrance floated the flag of Russia.

" It don't look much like a prison," said Scott.

" I believe, upon my word, that it's a palace," Roy added.

" Do you suppose these dummies are taking us to call upon the Tzar ? "

" I believe they are," Roy replied, as the door was opened by a fellow, all gold and lace, and they were evidently invited to follow him.

THE WINTER PALACE.

Through the massive portal they entered a grand corridor, glistening with marble and agate and gold; then up two flights of marble stairs and along another corridor, adorned with statues and bright with blue

enamel; turning to the right, then turning to the left, till they were utterly bewildered.

"They can't seem to find the Tzar," Scott whispered; "but it must be awkward to have to trot visitors all over the house to hunt him up."

" I believe it would have been cheaper to have walked up from the wharf and taken a carriage after we got here," Roy remarked as they still kept on and on.

" Don't you trouble yourself about economy, Roy," Scott whispered back. " The Tzar will be glad enough to pay the bills when he finds out who has come to see him."

At that moment they were ushered into a fine large room, with a grate fire roaring a welcome, with two little beds, several easy chairs, a table, a toilet room at one side and two long windows, so curiously guarded by awnings that they could see nothing but the sky.

As the door closed behind them and they were left alone, Scott turned to Roy. He could not help laughing at the solemn, anxious face he saw, and waving his hand exclaimed: .

" Sit down, Captain Sargent, and make yourself at home. The Tzar has stepped out for a moment. I reckon he's gone to the barn, for I see he's taken the milk pail along with him; but he'll be in directly. There ! "

There was a tap on the door.

" For mercy's sake, keep still, Scott ! " Roy whispered hurriedly, as the door opened and another individual all gold lace appeared, followed by two more who deposited a smoking breakfast upon the table.

" I don't see how they kept it so hot if they came up the way we did," Scott observed as they sat down and began to eat with excellent appetites.

On the second day after their arrival they were visited by three grand officials with clerks and papers and pens as well as an interpreter.

They were questioned carefully concerning themselves, from the cradle to Kronstadt, and everything was scrupulously committed to writing. It took so long that a great samova— a Russian contrivance for keeping tea at a boiling point — was brought in, and a tray of dried salt fish and crackers, and the officials ate and sipped and talked.

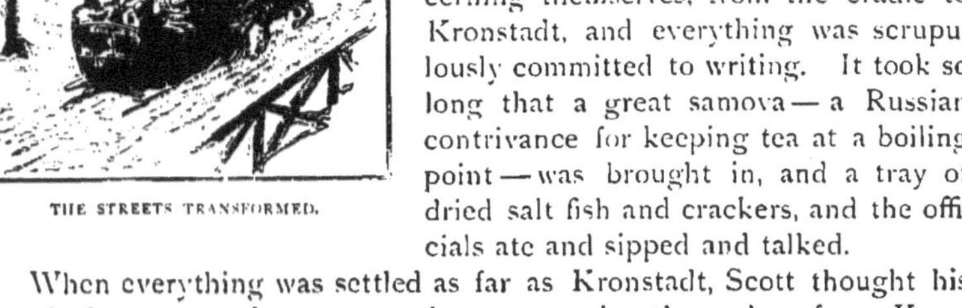

THE STREETS TRANSFORMED.

When everything was settled as far as Kronstadt, Scott thought his turn had come to ask some questions concerning themselves from Kronstadt on. His questions were all recorded, but not an answer could he obtain. Then Roy tried his hand, and said he supposed they had a right to communicate with some official of the American Legation. That too, was recorded, and the whole party bowed very politely and left them alone again.

"What's the use of talking to men like that, any way," Roy muttered.

"I expect we shall find out when they are ready to let us know, and I don't think we shall before," said Scott, looking up at the sky. "It's

AN OPEN FIRE AT THE STATION.

snowing like mad, Roy. Winter's set in, and no mistake. Wonder if the Tzar wouldn't accommodate us with a sleighride if we put it right. The streets are transformed. Hark! hear the sleighbells."

"I wish we had the *Snowbird* out of the Gulf of Finland," Roy muttered; but a week went by, and they had neither left their quarters nor heard a single word which they could understand.

At last, however, something happened. A man without any attending clerks or pens or ink came in alone, and seated himself beside the table. He was a plain, common-sense looking fellow, with silver strands in his hair and beard, but he seemed to be thoroughly accustomed to himself, and he spoke excellent English. The boys took a fancy to him at once.

"Young gentlemen," he said, " by a little accident some high officials

of the Russian Government became acquainted with the curious story which you told the magistrate at Kronstadt. They were interested, and resolved to investigate the matter. They have done so and are satisfied that you are right. Now they propose to aid you, if they can."

" Roy! didn't I tell you so?" burst unexpectedly from Scott's lips, and made him blush to the very roots of his hair.

"You were quite right, if you did," the visitor replied with a friendly smile. "Now they have learned this much: the man whom you represent as Captain Downing, reached Sebastopol, at the extreme south of Russia, about three months ago. The estates in question are chiefly located there. He had with him a young girl whom you represent as his daughter, whom he represents as a child adopted in infancy and heir to the estates. He presented as proof the family jewels belonging to her mother, the marriage certificate, birth record and sufficient other matter to convince the courts, and all the law allowed, in the time that has elapsed, of the property has been turned over to her. It will be necessary for us to take you, under a nominal guard, to Moscow, then to the estates to identify the two and have them summoned to an investi-

gation. If there are any questions which you wish to ask before I go I shall be glad to answer them."

"I'd like to know about the *Snowbird*, our vessel," said Roy. "She'll be frozen in before we can get back again if we leave her at Kronstadt.

"For that reason," replied the stranger, "she was dismantled four days ago, and is now being transported to Taganrog, on the Sea of

Azof. By the time you reach Sebastopol she will be floating in the fjord of Balaklava, a few miles away, precisely as you left her at Kronstadt, restocked with the best that Russia can supply, with your crew on board in charge of an officer who will remain with her till, at your pleasure, he has piloted you safely through the Bosporus, the Dardanelles and Sea of Marmora, when he will furnish you with proper papers to avoid any future contingency."

Scott was doubtful. He stood with his hands in his pockets, leaning against the wall. His head was a little on one side as he remarked:

"If you are making fun of us it is a mean thing to do."

The Russian simply smiled in the same friendly way, and replied:

"Necessity is the mother of invention. We have transported larger vessels than yours, bodily, from Kronstadt to Taganrog. If you have nothing else to ask I must bid you good-morning."

"I should like to know, sir, the name of this building where we have been so kindly cared for," Roy said as he took the stranger's proffered hand in parting.

"It is called 'The Winter Palace,'" he replied.

"And I," said Scott, "if it is not impertinent — I should like to know your name. To you, sir, or to some one, we owe a great deal."

"My name?" replied the stranger as he opened the door. "Really, I can hardly remember it myself. I am a most unenviable man, my friend — I am the Tzar. Good-morning, and God speed you."

The boys stood looking at each other. They were still standing and looking, and neither had spoken a word, when a man in gold lace appeared and conducted them to a coach, this time on runners, with four horses and outriders; and after all, the Tzar gave them a sleighride.

The horses flew over the frozen ground to the merry jangle of the bells, and as they drew up at the railway station they noticed a great fire blazing in the open square, fed by Government servants, about which a crowd was gathered, driving out the chills of early winter.

An engine and one car stood ready in the station, and the moment

A RUSSIAN MAIL SLEDGE.

they stepped on board with the official who was to accompany them, it started away like the wind for a run of four hundred miles to Moscow, straight as the crow flies, over a road laid out by the Emperor Nicholas. He came into the room when his engineers were quarreling and disputing over the twists and turns of a road between the two capitals which should accommodate itself to all the towns upon the way. Nicholas listened to their arguments for a moment, then caught up a ruler. With one end at St. Petersburg and the other at Moscow, as they appeared upon the map, he drew his pen along the edge.

"There," said he, "lay out your railroad along that line." And now the towns by the way accommodate themselves to the railroad instead.

All along the way, for the first hundred miles and more, the snow lay deep upon the ground. The stations were located as near the towns as the straight line allowed, but there were always long lines of sledges coming and going, connecting them with the towns.

RUSSIAN MAIL WAGON.

Near midnight, as they were approaching a station they passed a wealthy farmer or nobleman lying upon a sledge drawn by three horses abreast, while the driver stood up lashing the horses and shouting, evidently mistaking the special for the midnight express and fearing that his master would be left.

The mail was brought to the stations upon curious sledges, which sometimes made a journey of nearly a hundred miles. Once, coming from a little village not more than a mile away, they passed a woman, bringing the mail upon a miniature coach, drawn by a pair of huge mastiffs, wallowing through the snow.

JEWEL VAULT.

"Scott Campbell," said Roy, "do you realize that we have been to St. Petersburg and gone away without setting foot upon a single street, or knowing the name of a single building, church, gallery, museum or college, except the Winter Palace?"

"Who cares?" said Scott. "Ten thousand Yankees have known them all; but I am an Esquimau if I don't believe that they would swap the whole, twice over, to spend a week in the Winter Palace, and chat and shake hands with that unenviable man the Tzar."

As they rolled along there were many questions to ask, but the official refused to pay the slightest heed to anything but their requirements of rest and refreshment. They crossed the four hundred miles of forests and marshes, left the winter far behind them and entered the almost Oriental city of Moscow.

There a carriage was again in waiting, and again, like Jehu the driver drove furiously; but two pairs of bright, sharp eyes saw a great deal of the famous old capital of Russia in a short, quick drive. First, they crossed a great stone bridge, upon a series of graceful arches, with the Kremlin in full view; a walled city, in itself two miles in circumference, in the very heart of the great city of Moscow.

Within that inner wall rose churches, palaces, monasteries, arsenals, art galleries and museums with grandly decorated walls and towers, domes and spires, flashing with gold, glistening in enamel.

THE KREMLIN, MOSCOW.

As they crossed the bridge, and the carriage rolled under a magnificent arched gateway to enter this inner city, the driver removed his hat, the officer followed his example, and indicated to the boys that they must do the same. They obeyed, without knowing that above their heads, pro-

THE GREAT BELL.

tected by the overhanging of the arch, was a picture of the Saviour, and that they were entering the Kremlin by the Redeemer's Gate.

The Tzars are crowned within the Kremlin, and from the emperor to the meanest peasant every one removes his hat, and with uncovered head passes through that Redeemer's Gate.

Upon their left rose the narrow but substantial tower, marking the Royal Jewel Vault. They were scarcely beyond it when something met their eyes which gave them a peculiar shock — like suddenly coming upon an old friend in the midst of the Sahara Desert. They had traversed one quarter of Russia without knowing the name of a single object which met their gaze, when suddenly they came upon something

in bewildering Moscow, which they knew as well as the boy born and
bred within sight of it. It was the Tzar Kolokol, the Great Bell of Mos-
cow. They had seen it in their geographies and illustrated readers.
They had looked at it a hundred times. They knew all about it; that
it was more than twenty feet high; that it weighed four hundred
thousand pounds; that its metal alone was worth over two million dol-
lars. And here it was, just like its pictures, looming up for an instant to
greet them as they dashed past it.

They only drove through the Kremlin, leaving it again by the St.
Nicholas Gate, and out upon a broad road and a great square, with the
wall of the Kremlin upon their right. There was a bronze group upon
a rose-granite pedestal in the center of the street, with public buildings

ST. NICHOLAS GATE.

in every direction, and other streets as broad leading away in the most
fantastic irregularity imaginable.

They crossed the square, toward perhaps the most remarkable church
on earth. It was, in reality, the Cathedral of Basil the Blessed, but in
utter ignorance the boys watched it till the carriage stopped.

CATHEDRAL OF BASIL THE BLESSED.

It was one grand chaos of angles, towers and domes ; no two alike in shape or size or color; of all kinds of material and all styles of architecture ; a marvel, however one looked at it.

The boys had only to go through a peculiar legal ceremony, and place their signatures upon papers already prepared, when they were

APPROACHING THE CATHEDRAL.

hurried back to their car again, which started at once for the south.

Like a meteor, Moscow, the wealthiest of Russian cities, flashed before them, and in the flame expired, but they were too anxious to reach the distant Crimea to care how brief their stay had been.

CHAPTER X.

ON TO BALAKLAVA!

AS their car waited at a little station south of Tula for a train to the
north to pass, they saw the mounted Cossacks forcing back the
starving peasants who were making a weak effort to leave the village, in
the vague hope of finding something somewhere, while in curious con-
trast, on a bench upon the sunny side of the station, a group of children
had gathered, and were singing away as though their lives depended on
the amount of noise they made. One fellow was beating time, and
another was playing on two fifes at once.

At another station, while they were taking wood and water, they
watched a group of peasants waiting for their share of a car-load of coarse
flour and meal that was standing upon a side track, being dispensed by
Government officials.

They had little opportunity to know of the internal disturbances of
which the world at large was constantly supplied with graphically
distorted and wondrously exaggerated details.

A group of ragged and disconsolate Jews, sitting on the ground to
rest while they waited for the train to pass, recalled the unfortunate lot
of the children of Israel in the empire, and more than once the destitute
condition of some famine-stricken district appeared for an instant and
was gone. That was all that they knew either of the persecution of the
Jews or the terrors of the famine. Perhaps it was really all there was to
know, or perhaps it was simply intended that they should not know.

They were only catching glimpses cf a great reality in Russia, much as they had caught glimpses of those other realities, St. Petersburg and Moscow, and in time the car crossed the narrow isthmus, entered the peninsular of Crimea and stood in the station of Sebastopol.

Here, to their surprise, they discovered that the officer who had accompanied them could speak very fair English.

"The old reprobate!" Scott muttered. "He didn't mean that we should bother him with questions. That's what's the matter."

"And upon my word, I think he was rather bright," Roy replied, thinking how he would have plied the poor official, and kept him talking.

"Wonder if we said much that was out of order?" Scott queried.

"Presume so," Roy replied. "We generally do under such circumstances. But he has himself to blame if he didn't like to hear us call him 'Rushy.'"

The officer had explained to them that there was a large house

THE RUSSIAN CHILDREN'S SONG.

belonging to the estates in Sebastopol, and a large farm and country-house some two miles back upon the hills toward Balaklava, and had left them to wait while he made inquiries to learn where the supposed Captain Downing could be found.

"Toward Balaklava!" said Scott. "That's where the *Snowbird* was to wait for us."

"Whatever have we heard at home about Balaklava?" Roy asked, scratching his head, in the sailor's inevitable gesture of thought.

He was still thinking when Scott suddenly struck a tragic attitude, and throwing out one hand exclaimed :

> " ' Forward, the light brigade !
> Charge for the guns !' he said.

That's Balaklava, Roy.   Hope we shall get a good peep at it."

A pretty Circassian girl, with a long, slender rod in her hand and a basket on her arm, came up and, smiling, opened the basket, out of which hopped several little birds.   Looking up she said, in English :

HOLDING BACK THE STARVING PEASANTS.

" Fine gentlemen, fine fortune. Me little birds tells fortunes true."

There is always a peculiar fascination about gypsies, and a peculiar fascination to the sailor about having his fortune told. There is always an irresistible charm in one's own language, when one meets it unex-pectedly, and Scott, in his impulsive prodi-gality, put a gold piece in her hand. It was a Swedish coin, but it was all he had, and gold is gold the wide world over.

She smiled, held out the rod, and two of the birds lit upon one end of it. She stood silently watching them. One began to hop away, and the other followed. The last one almost caught up and gave the first a peck, but he jumped away, and the last lost his balance, and would have fallen off the rod, but for the help of his wings. They kept it up till they reached the end of the rod; then the first, grasping it in his feet, hung down, head-first, as though he were dead. A third bird flew up from the basket, lit on the end of the rod, and looked for a mo-ment at the bird which had been following. The two exchanged a lit-tle bird's kiss, and all three flew back to the basket.

WAITING FOR RATIONS.

"So it is," said the pretty fortune teller. "One runs away, another follows. Sometimes he come near enough to peck, but almost fall, and only white wings save him. He come to sad end. He can't help. But one sweet kiss and all is bright. God bless young gentlemen," and she walked away.

" You remember the hawk that fell dead upon the deck, at the very moment when we were laying our course to Greenland? " said Roy.

" Well? " said Scott.

" Well, that was a fool's errand. Captain Downing hadn't gone that way."

" Oh! fudge, Roy. It was a queer coincidence, but "—

" And when the end comes this gypsy's birds may be another," Roy interrupted.

Scott was about to laugh at Roy's superstition when the officer drove up in a post-troika, with a burly Russian seated behind the horses.

wrapped in a thick coat, though it was very warm, and wearing a hat which Scott declared beat all creation.

They drove out two miles toward Balaklava, six miles beyond.

The country seat was certainly magnificent, but the great gate upon the street was locked, and no porter was in the lodge.

They were obliged to leave the troika and walk nearly a quarter of a mile through the park to the stately mansion.

The servant who came to the door assured them that the master and lady had driven to Sebastopol, to return the evening of the next day.

It was dark when they reached Sebastopol again, but the same story was repeated at the city mansion: they were not there.

" It may be they have gone to Odessa," said the servant. " I do not think the yacht *Vera* is in the bay."

" So the estate possesses a yacht, too," Roy muttered, " and her name is *Vera*. I wonder what has come over Louise that she is taking part in this?"

" In some way she doesn't know what she's doing, I'll bet on that," said Scott, and he felt Roy give his hand a squeeze.

They held a council and decided ·o again to the country seat. �archeᴗ in the morning, and wait ' ᴀrn of the ca;·tai· ᴠ.

A ·n they were oblig·d ·ᴐ leave the troika at the gate, but this tᴗᴍc they were invited in and told to entertain themselves in a large drawing-room, where a samova of steaming tea was placed for them.

" A BURLY RUSSIAN."

" If he had been in the house and seen us coming, do you think he would make himself scarce ? " Roy asked; and as Scott was about to answer his ear caught the sound of distant wheels.

It was difficult to see through the dense foliage of the park, but straining his eyes, between the branches he was sure that he saw their troika, with a man and woman seated in it, moving away behind an-

THE FORTUNE TELLER.

other loaded with something like trunks. "Come quick!" he exclaimed, and sprang to the door followed by Roy and the fat official. They ran down the road to the gate. Their troika was gone!

"This way!" cried Scott, starting toward Balaklava.

Roy and Scott ran side by side, and soon left the puffing officer lagging behind. The boys were strong and determined, but a sailor's life pays little attention to the legs, and theirs were ready to give out when they came upon a three-horse hay cart, into which a peasant, at some distance, was laboriously gathering a little crop of grain, grown in famine year.

"It's our only chance!" Scott exclaimed. "We can make it right afterward. Jump in, Roy, and jump quick."

Like a flash the boys were in the hay cart. Scott caught the whip and gave the horses a cut. They started at a furious rate, for they were Russians, while the poor peasant stared in blank astonishment.

"Glory hallelujah!" Scott gasped. "See there! On the next hill! There's the troika! Who knows but we can overhaul it!"

"If they know whose aboard this crib they'll hurry, and if they do they can outrun these lean things two to one," said Roy.

"Good idea!" Scott replied, catching up the peasant's coat and hat lying in the cart, and putting them on. "There! If I'm not a Russian, what am I? Gee up, there!" he shouted. "Now, Captain Sargent, just you lie low. Stow yourself away among that straw. Keep clean out of sight. I've got three sails to their two. any way. Gee up, there! and if I don't overhaul that brig it's 'cause there ain't wind enough in the sails, or 'cause I don't understand this steering gear. Gee up!"

"I'd give more for two jibs like the cobs that brought us up, than for ten acres of these condemned old war-horses," Roy replied from down among the straw.

"Never you mind!" Scott cried. "We're gaining on her! Gee up! This lash seems to speak first-class Russian, and I reckon the handle understands English, for it translates what I'm after. Gee up!"

"For mercy's sake," groaned Roy, as they splashed through a lot of water and banged over a wooden bridge, "you'll smash everything to pieces, Scott."

"I reckon I may, Captain," Scott replied. "To tell the truth — gee up, there! — I'm not just sure of the hull of this craft, nor of the tackle either — gee up! — and the rigging is the doubtfullest stuff I ever handled. Gee up! But I — whew! We near went to pieces on that rock."

"So we did," groaned Roy.

"Guess she's got a stronger bottom than I thought for — gee up! gee up!"

"Are you in the road at all?" Roy asked.

"Don't know, Captain." Scott replied. "I've got my eye on the craft ahead, and can't keep it in two places at once. Gee up! We're gaining — gee up! — or I'm an Esquimau — gee up! And I don't believe I'd know the road if I watched for it. There don't seem to be any

unless it's all in Russian and I can't make it out. Gee up, there! And I couldn't tell how to keep in it, if I could see it plain as my nose — gee up! — for there's only one line apiece running out to the prow of each of these animals, like the reindeer in Lapland. Gee up, there! When I pull they slow up so I let 'em lie loose and use the whip. Gee up! If the lash don't come off I'll keep 'em going till something splits. Gee up! Cracky! but that was a bad bump. Is there any water in the hold? Seem's though we must have sprung aleak that time. Gee up! gee up! gee up! Jehu! They've struck a new tack and bust my best cable, but they're gaining! Gee up!"

"How are they now?" Roy asked a moment later.

"Can't just say; they're round a curve. Gee up! I believe these things are getting used to the whip, or else the wind's giving out. Gee up! Never mind, we'll be going down hill again in a minute.

BALAKLAVA.

That's our best tack, for there don't seem to be any hold-backs about the rigging, and they have to run like mad to keep the crib off their heels. There! Didn't I tell you? Gee up! or we'll run over you!"

"I say, Scott, this thing is listing to port like everything. Do you know where you're going?"

"Going to Balaklava, Captain. May be we're listing, but I don't see why. Everything's level on ahead. The horses know the road better than I do. Guess they smell the town. At any rate, they act as though they thought they were going somewhere and one of them — gee up, there! — seems to think he's almost there — gee up! — but we are listing, no mistake. I believe — G. Whittaker! — There! I told you so. Any bones broken? No? Glad of that. It wasn't my fault," Scott said, as he pulled Roy out of a mass of straw and dirt and fragments of a Russian hay cart. " I had my mouth open to say that I believed a wheel was coming off."

" Well, you would have been mighty near right, Scott," said Roy, rubbing several bruises, while Scott brushed off the dirt and straw as they stood beside the dilapidated wreck. " I wish that gypsy and her birds had kept away."

" Bother the gypsy!" Scott exclaimed. " It was the wheel came off, and if the birds did have anything to do with it, why, the white wings of the *Snowbird* may save us yet. Don't forget that she's at Balaklava if we need her. Come on!

> ' Forward, the light brigade!'
> Bother the gypsy maid!' "

And setting the example, he began to run again.

They reached the summit of the next hill. The troikas were out of sight, but there, in the valley before them, lay the town of Balaklava, the oldest city in Russia — old as the days of Ulysses; governed in turn by Italians, Greeks, Turks and Russians; with its dilapidated fortresses and ruined breastworks; its ragged mountains and deep and silent fjord. And there they saw the white-winged *Snowbird*.

" Come on," cried Scott.

Roy tried to, but fell back again.

"Scott, I can't!" he muttered. " I'm dizzy. I can't stand up. My heart is beating terribly."

" Well, you just stop and rest and come on easy," said Scott. " I'll bet I have strength enough left to reach that wharf, and I want to make sure what Captain Downing's up to. Good-by! Come on easy."

Late that afternoon the Russian officer and Roy rescued Scott from the filth of the Balaklava jail.

His story was quickly told. He had met Captain Downing upon the wharf, after one boat loaded with boxes and carrying Louise, had reached the yacht which lay at anchor there.

The captain attempted to escape him, but Scott, too much exhausted to speak, caught him by the coat.

" Scott Campbell!" he exclaimed, "you will touch me at your own peril. You know who you are dealing with. I advise you to go back to

America and hold your tongue. I am going to Constantinople for a while, where I shall be out of reach of you, of Russia or America. If you keep still I'll make it for your interest. I'll make you rich. If you don't I'll be the death of you. There! Let go!"

"I never would have let go," said Scott, "though I couldn't speak a word to save my life, but who should come up but the everlasting fossil

OUTSIDE THE FJORD.

who belonged to that hay cart. He'd come over the hills by a short cut. He accused me of I don't know what. Then he pointed to his coat and hat. I had forgotten that I had them on. I declare, I don't know what did happen, after that. I don't believe I fainted, but I didn't know much till I found myself in here. Now the quicker we get to Constantinople the better."

CHAPTER XI.

THE officer telegraphed for instructions and received reply:

"Follow to Constantinople. Report and await orders."

So the *Snowbird* sailed away, bounding over the waves of the Black Sea as gracefully as upon the Arctic Ocean. The boys found the Russian who had brought her from Kronstadt as jovial a fellow as he was a good sailor, and they very willingly gave the command of the *Snowbird* into his hands, finding that they enjoyed themselves infinitely more when relieved of the keen edge of anxious responsibility.

They had need of the free and independent use of all their eyes and all their wits, for there is no point from which the magnificent city of the Mussulmans appears to such glorious advantage as when from the Black Sea one enters the Bosporus and approaches the Golden Horn.

On one hand Scutari rose, backed by Asiatic hills, on the other Galata and Pera the Frankish cities, and Stamboul the great Turkish city in the center, all doing their utmost to make one great, glorious Constantinople.

No one ever had a better opportunity to see the Moslem city from the bay, for the captain and the officer who had accompanied the boys, keeping a sharp lookout, ran the *Snowbird* the entire length of the harbor. At last they sighted the *Pera*, with all sail set, moving out of the bay. They overhauled her, and in the name of the Tzar boarded and searched her. All they learned was that the *Vera* was ordered to return to Russia and go into winter quarters at Balaklava. The captain found that he was in danger of arrest and punishment, however, and confessed that he had placed a large amount of luggage and his two passengers upon a steamer bound for Alexandria and the way ports on the coast of Syria. After that he was allowed to sail away.

"We must go on at once!" Scott exclaimed.

"If you wish," replied the captain. "The vessel is yours, and my orders are to see you safely as far as the Mediterranean. Then I must leave you. The officer's orders are to go to Constantinople, report and wait commands. He must stay here. If you will allow me to suggest, however, when Russia becomes interested in discovering and checking

CONSTANTINOPLE.

crime she stops at nothing. If you are willing to wait for orders, here, I think they will be such as will assist you."

"I think we'd better wait, then," Scott replied, and Roy, as ever a little more deliberate, brought up the rear with his usual, "Me, too."

It was early in the morning. They were relieved of responsibility on land as well as sea, and while the officer was telegraphing, Roy and Scott went on shore to see what they could of Constantinople. A signal was to be run up on the *Snowbird* when orders were received, and till then they were free to wander where they would.

For two hours they wandered aimlessly about the great Mohammedan

THE SNOWBIRD IN THE HARBOR.

capital, satisfied only to see and see and see the ever-changing panorama; domes and minarets, mosques and palaces; narrow streets and grand boulevards; markets and bazaars where people of all nations were clamoring in a babel of voices; costumes and faces from every clime and country on the earth, except the fur clothing of the North; churches, hospitals, colleges, factories, all crowding upon the shores of the Bosporus.

"I never dreamed of anything like this in all my life," said Roy. "Why! there are no two minutes alike. We are going downhill, then uphill. We are on a level road, then we are climbing a long flight of stone steps with front doors opening upon either side all the way. Now the street is so wide a dozen carriages could go abreast; a moment ago we could touch the houses on both sides at once. We have walked through mud and dust and sand, and now look at this fine pavement. We have had to walk in the middle of the street because there was nothing but middle; not a sign of a sidewalk, and there is a street, upon my word, that is nothing but sidewalk, with just a little gutter in the center. You go through a street so crowded that you have to shoulder your way, and the next you know you are out in the suburbs, catching on bushes growing in the path, with a lot more city just beyond. You hold your nose to save it from smells viler than Lapland and Fiskenaes combined, and the first you know the air is like the attar of roses from gardens on either side."

"Hold up a minute, Roy, and look at that fellow coming along with a jug. Jehu! what a face. If he had milk in there I'll bet it would sour before it grew cold. See him giving that fellow a drink. Oh! it's water; and he's taking pay for it. He's a sort of walking soda fountain."

"JEHU! WHAT A FACE."

"There's another fellow round the corner at the same trade. Now I think of it we've seen lots of them. It must be a good business or there'd not be so many; but for my part I'd rather go dry."

"What's the matter with the fellow's eye? Do you suppose he's had a crack, or is it only a fashionable tip he has on his turban."

"O, Scott! look at that little chappie riding horseback! My! isn't he a beauty!"

" Mind the tassel on his fez though ! and his little pug nose. He's a swell of some sort. Wish I knew his name."

" Look here, Scott. Here we are out on the brow of a hill, looking down on the harbor. However did we come here? In five minutes more — there ! what did I tell you — quicker, even, we are in this narrow, dirty alley, full of vile smells, filthy beggars "—

" Look at the baby roosting on that fellow's shoulder ! You'd think he was wanting to shake hands, but I suppose it's money he's after."

" What a Babylon Constantinople is !" said Roy.

" But it's beautiful ! wonderfully beautiful !" Scott exclaimed.

" And ugly ! ugh ! horribly ugly !" Roy added.

" You don't like it," Scott said.

" Indeed I do, madly ! And you ? "

Scott shook his head. They were each radically inconsistent, of course ; but every one is inconsistent in Constantinople. and all together are not half so inconsistent as Constantinople's self.

They were half-sliding down a steep hill, along the slimy pavement of a narrow alley, at the end of which they came out upon a broader street and a floating bridge stretching across the narrowest part of the Golden Horn.

" For mercy's sake, Roy, stop a bit ! " Scott exclaimed, catching his arm. " Just look at this crowd ! What in the name of wonder are they all and where are they going ? "

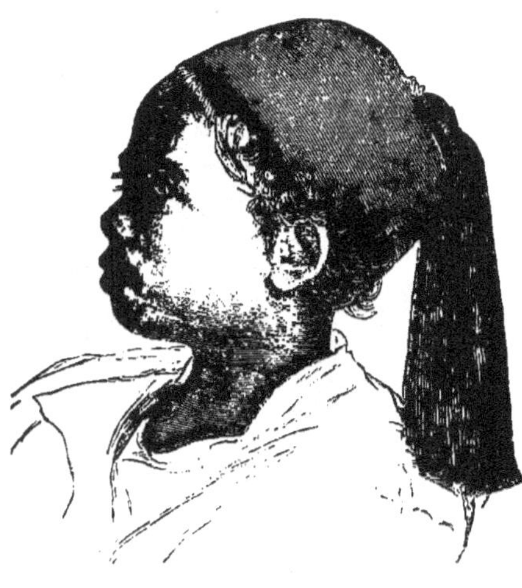

" ISN'T HE A BEAUTY."

" From Europe to Asia or coming back," Roy replied deliberately, as he watched that interminable throng of human beings, that for ages has made the floating bridge of the Golden Horn one of the wonders of the world.

" It's a pretty big thing to do on one small bridge," Scott mused.

IN THE MOSQUE OF ST. SOPHIA.

" See that woman with only two eyes sticking through her veil ? "

" How many eyes would you expect to find sticking through one woman's veil ? " Roy asked.   " See those porters trotting along with big

" SEE THAT WOMAN ! "

bales upon their backs, and there are four fellows carrying a monster on a pole between them.   They don't seem to have any drays or truck-teams here."

" Well, they surely have surplus backs enough to carry everything, and there are precious few streets where a truck-team could navigate."

"Great Scott!" Roy gasped, catching Scott by the arm, "is that a storm cloud or the ace of spades?"

"I reckon it's the Moor of Venice, lost his way home. He 'pears to be looking for something," Scott replied, as a huge fellow from Zanzibar lounged leisurely through the crowd. He was black as black could be, and in the curious characteristic of extremes which marks humanity the wide world over, where it follows natural inclinations and not the artifice

"THE ACE OF SPADES."

of fashion, he was wrapped from head to foot in a robe of muslin as white as the driven snow.

Then they wandered away and into the Mosque of St. Sophia. Here and there among its massive pillars, people were kneeling on little mats, barefooted, always facing in one direction, bowing, bending forward, touching their foreheads to the ground. In another part of the mosque white-haired and long-bearded fellows sat upon the floor, with open books on little desks before them, shouting and gesticulating to curiously dressed men lying on the floor about them.

"Maybe this is a Mohammedan Sunday-school," Scott suggested. There was no way for them to find out that really they had come very near the truth. The Mohammedan holy day is Friday, but without regard to that teachers always sit at those little desks, expounding the Koran to any who will come and listen.

Then they wandered on again, and in ten minutes were in an entirely different quarter from anything which they had seen before. Houses, dress, faces, language — everything seemed changed.

IN THE ALGERIAN QUARTER.

" Look at that fellow on the corner, smoking a cigarette. If he's not a Spaniard what is he?' Roy asked.

" He's no one I'm acquainted with," said Scott. " Let's see, we ought to know an Esquimau, or a Lapp, or a Swede, or a Norwegian or Russian by this time, but out of all this jumble I'm blest if I have any idea how a Turk looks or what he is."

" Not like that, any way, I'm sure," said Roy, pointing to a little girl standing in a low door, with her head on one side, and a baby balanced on her back.

The fact is, they had entered a quarter inhabited almost entirely by Algerians and Spanish ; a little oasis where not a shadow of the Moslem city fell ; and Scott was not far from right in wondering what the real Turk was and where he could be found.

The question was soon answered for him, however, when they turned again toward the wharves, and this time found themselves wandering through the mazes of Stamboul — the real Constantinople.

Even here there was a constant mingling of all sorts of foreign elements, but the majority was Turkish, through and through.

There were rich and poor ; carriages, coaches, sedan chairs and palanquins ; rags, tatters and silks ; jewels and dirt crowding all about them as they entered the great bazaar of Stamboul.

A SPANIARD.

" I've heard of bazaars of the Orient before," said Roy, " but I never expected to see a real live one. What a bewildering affair it is ! "

"I've heard of the dogs of Constantinople before, but I've seen more dogs to-day than in all my life before.   Look at those gaunt fellows lying there.   What a forlorn set they are," Scott added.

"A CHARACTER."

"Seems to me everything and everybody is forlorn," Roy replied. "Think of how every one was laughing all the time up in Greenland and Lapland.   And here no one seems to laugh at all."

"We thought them half-idiots for their perpetual grins," said Scott, "but I declare, it makes us sober, too — these long faces.   Wonder if it's the effect of the Tropics?   Think of the lark we had with the Lapps.   Why, we couldn't have anything of the sort here."

"That's so," Roy added.   "If it grows worse as we go south I shall be blue as indigo before long.   Hope we shall soon be able to turn about again."

It did grow worse as they went south, and the discovery they had already made became a confirmed fact that has perplexed the brain of many a wiser traveler.   From the pole to the equator the smile becomes less pronounced and less frequent, no matter what line of longitude one follows southward.

"Look at that fellow, now, with a white petticoat down to his knees, with a turban twisted round his fez, and a big sash for a girdle, full of swords and pistols.   Wonder what that spike he's carrying is used for?

How his slippers turn up at the toes!   But bless me! you'd think he'd lost his last friend by the looks of his face.   I tell you, he's a character."

IN THE BAZAAR.

" Hold on!   Here's a shop with fezzes for sale.   I'm going to invest," said Scott, and Roy echoed: " Me, too."

While they were purchasing, Scott gave Roy a little nudge and pointed through an open door.   In an inner room, a woman sat upon a

THROUGH THE OPEN DOOR.

sofa, smoking a hookah.   It was a large vase, with a bowl at the top, holding the lighted tobacco, and water beneath, through which the smoke passed into a long, twisting tube which she held in her hand, with a beautiful amber mouthpiece.

" Ladies don't seem to think anything more against smoking here than in Greenland and Lapland, but I can't get used to it," said Roy.

" Isn't it a handsome costume, though ? " Scott whispered.   " I guess she's a Greek.   See! the name of the place is in letters that look kind of Greeky."

"And just see that little tot sitting on the floor," said Roy.

"Oh! isn't she a beauty?" Scott cried, in his enthusiasm. "Isn't she pretty? I never saw such a face before. I wonder if she is a Greek,

"THOSE EYES ARE SAD."

too. If she is I wish we could go to Greece, and spend a month there."

" But those big black eyes are sad, just like all the rest of them," Roy continued. " I believe I'm growing homesick. I want to get away and feel the deck of the *Snowbird* beneath my feet once more. Come on, it's time we're moving."

They made a few more purchases, then turned toward the wharves, where they found they had more than two miles to walk before reaching a point near the *Snowbird*.

All the way the endless variety of Constantinople continued.

"I believe one could see almost the whole world here in half an hour," Roy remarked. "I'm sure we've met people from Spain and Italy; from Greece and Russia; from Asia and Africa " —

"Come, pa, get a gait on and hustle! If you don't brace up we'll get left," cried a curly-headed boy, laughing, as he pulled his father through the crowd.

"And from America, I'll be bound," Scott added to Roy's unfinished

"TAKE YOUR LAST PEEP AT CONSTANTINOPLE."

sentence, at which Roy shrugged his shoulders, for he was not so fond as Scott, of that vernacular which so often distinguishes his countrymen abroad.

When the Russians returned to the *Snowbird* the boys learned that everything was arranged to their best advantage. Captain Downing had taken everything available in plate, jewels and money from the estate. The Government was convinced that he was a fraud, and directed the two officers to continue with the boys, and render every possible assistance in arresting and returning the fugitives, or securing the wealth they had carried away.

" I'd like to see the fellow who dares say anything to me against the Tzar of Russia," Scott exclaimed, tossing his head under his new fez, and pulling up one sleeve a little as he stood by the helm ready to turn the *Snowbird* to the wind when the anchor floated.

" You're right," said Roy; " but while you're about it, take your last peep at Constantinople. Who knows when or how we shall ever see it again ? "

So they saw their first and last of Constantinople, and turned their faces again toward the dancing waves of the beautiful bay beyond, where sails were darting to and fro. They were already anxious to be with them.

THE BEAUTIFUL BAY.

CHAPTER XII.

THE anchor rose, the sails filled, the *Snowbird* passed through the Hellespont where Leander swam, and out of the Dardanelles, with her white wings spread to their utmost capacity. The sheathing had been taken off her bows, and all the marks of ice obliterated by a coat of paint, while crossing Russia. Her broken gear had all been replaced with new, and a prettier little vessel never sailed the waters of the Levant.

" I suppose we should follow the steamer into every port where she stopped," said the captain; and Roy and Scott agreeing, he made the first landing at Smyrna.

At the head of a long bay the little city of Smyrna lies nestling at the base of a mountain. Its white walls and flat roofs shone in the sunlight as they approached, in sharp contrast with the dense green about them and the black water at their base, making a picture so attractive that the boys longed to go on shore, and even suggested going on to the ruins of the great city of Ephesus, beyond the hills, where the gorgeous temple of Diana stood, a little inland from Smyrna. But distance gave enchantment to the view, and nearness took it away again.

By the time they reached the stone pier the beauty was all gone. Narrow streets and filthy alleys, half of them arched over the top, where the houses met for mutual support, were the reality of the pretty picture they had been watching.

From the deck they saw enough of Smyrna, and fortunately did not penetrate those damp alleys, where half-naked natives, men, women and children, sit, with their backs against the walls, kneading and rolling figs all day long. The figs have been picked and dried, and must be rolled

SMYRNA.

and crushed and softened again to be packed for Western markets. Among the stores taken on at Smyrna were several boxes of those famous figs, and as the boys did not see the process of preparing them for boxing, they enjoyed the fruit.

Beyroot was their next stopping place. And that, too, was beautiful from the bay. It lay in a half-circle under the shelter of mountains, and with the glass the boys obtained their first glimpse of the great ships of the desert, as a caravan came over the hills toward the city from Damascus.

It was a fascinating picture, and as the boys stood watching it through the telescope, Scott exclaimed:

"I'm going to have a camel ride before I leave this part of the world, see if I don't!"

"You may have more than you bargain for, I'm thinking," Roy replied. "What if Captain Downing strikes for the interior?"

"We strike after him, I suppose. It's through Arctics and Tropics, isn't it?" said Scott.

"Of course it is," Roy answered; "but how little we knew of what was before us when we made that compact."

"We don't know much of what's before us now," Scott suggested.

"But we know an everlasting lot about what's behind us that was before us then, and somehow I'm not half so nervous now as I was before we rooted him out of his hole."

"That's so," said Scott decidedly. "He's running away now, and

LOADING THE CATTLE.

it's not half so uncertain following a fellow who's running from you as it is coming up to a fellow hidden somewhere behind a wall."

At their next stopping place, while the officer made his inquiries the boys watched a scow filled with Syrian cattle, run alongside of a steamer bound to Constantinople.

The deck was nearly twelve feet above the scow.

"I wonder how they'll manage to ship those creatures," Roy remarked; but his curiosity was soon satisfied by a scene of fiendish cruelty which is practiced every day along that coast, to supply the markets of Turkey from the green pastures of Syria.

The steamer's derrick chain was lowered, the hook was fastened in a strong rope tied round the animal's horns, and the steam turned on. The cow was caught up from the scow by her head, swung out in mid air, pulled over the deck and lowered into the cattle pen, between decks.

As the poor creatures banged against the side of the steamer sometimes a horn would break and they would drop back again, when the rope would be put around their necks, and once more the engine would pull them up.

In the peculiar fascination of anything horrible, the boys stood watching, till Scott, pale and excited, muttered:

"If I only had the power, I'd hang every brute on that deck to the yard arm and see how he liked it," and with that he turned and went into the cabin.

EPHESUS.

"Jaffa is our next stop, and there we shall land," said the officer, as they set sail again. "The steamer we passed is the one they took. She's made a quick passage. They went to Alexandria and returned to Jaffa, where they left the steamer; but they landed only two boxes with them, and have none on board. They must have disposed of the rest in some way at Alexandria."

Jaffa is the old Bible town of Joppa. It has always been one of the most important ports of Syria, but has the poorest harbor in the world. Two miles from the landing they were obliged to drop anchor; but necessity is the mother of invention, and a large navy of flat-bottomed boats lay about the walls of Jaffa, ready to dodge among the rocks, over the breakwater on the top of a wave, and place themselves at the service of every visitor.

The boys with the two Russians took the first boat to reach them. The captain of the surf boat was a wild, cadaverous-looking Arab, but

BEYROOT AND THE SHIPS OF THE DESERT.

making a frantic struggle to smile he said to Roy, who was nearest him:

"Musstakee guide. Fuss-class guide, me. Speakee fuss-class English. Here, you! Uppee dere Simmontannerous. Bottom side, big one rock, Jonah sittee down when whale spittee out. Fuss-class guide, me."

Scott caught the side of the boat and laughed till the tears rolled down his face. Roy turned to him, remarking:

"I say, Scott, if there's a joke in sight half-big enough for that I wish you'd explain it. I couldn't make out a word."

JAFFA.

THE CAPTAIN.

"Why, Roy, where's all your Sunday-school training? Our friend here declared that he was a first-class guide and spoke first-class English, and to prove it he stated that one of the buildings on yonder height was Simon the Tanner's house, and that the big rock out there was where Jonah landed when the whale spit him out. I've half a mind to hire him."

"If you want to act as interpreter, go ahead," Roy replied, as the boat drew up at a flight of slimy and green stone steps, leading up to the custom house.

While the Russians were making the necessary inquiries, Scott and Roy stood side by side as usual, looking in every direction.

Almost the first object to attract their attention was another water-carrier, shouting at the top of his lungs, but never looking up to see whether any one heard him or not.

"I wonder what he is saying," Roy remarked, when a young Jew standing near them replied: "He is only repeating the usual water-carrier's cry: 'Ho! ye who are thirsty! Here is wine and milk all for nothing!'"

"He got that out of the Bible!" Scott exclaimed.

"On the contrary," replied the Jew, "the Prophet Isaiah borrowed the water-carrier's cry to begin his grandest appeal to the people."

"Does he expect people to believe that he has wine and milk?" Roy asked.

"Oh! by no means," said the Jew. "It is only a cus-

THE INEVITABLE.

tom. If he had dates to sell he would cry figs, because they are better."

" That is a curious custom," said Scott.

" It seems to be old as the hills, but I reckon it's about the way people advertise in our papers at home," Roy suggested.

By this time the Russians came up, and they adjourned to a room in the inn of Jaffa, to consult.

A beggar sat at the inn door to welcome them. He received their coins without a sign of thanks, but they were too much in haste to care.

"AT THE INN DOOR."

Captain Downing and his daughter had arrived, and had gone to Jerusalem, three days before. They had evidently gone to Alexandria, as a blind, in case they were followed. They had left most of their luggage there, and the officer suspected they had shipped it upon some steamer through the Red Sea, to India, Ceylon or Australia, intending to follow it by some other route, and go on in that way to America.

" We can follow the luggage or follow them." he said.

" Where the treasure is there will the heart be," Roy repeated. " They will certainly come to their trunks and boxes some time."

JERUSALEM FROM MOUNT OF OLIVES.

"Why not follow both?" Scott suggested.

"How?" Roy asked.

"Why, we can go to Jerusalem and find out how they head, if we can't find them, and the *Snowbird* can take the captain and officer to

THE TOWER OF RAMLEH.

Alexandria and see where the luggage went. If it turns out as we suspect we can go overland and the captain by the Red Sea."

"Good idea!" Roy exclaimed, slapping Scott on the shoulder. The Russians also approved, and the boys started at once for Jerusalem, leaving the *Snowbird* to wait their arrival there before sailing.

The moon was rising as they passed the famous old tower of Ramleh, where so many crusaders lie buried. They could not sleep. Who could, during his first journey in the Holy Land? The serious element was yet lacking, for the various places of historic interest failed to possess more than a semblance of reality; still it was all wonderful, to be passing through the plain of Sharon, the valley where Samson set the three hundred foxes free in the ripening grain, with fire brands on their tails, the huts of Kirjath-jearim where the Ark of the Covenant rested, the village where the penitent thief was born, the birthplace of John the Baptist, the hills where Saul fought the Philistines, the valley of Ajalon where Joshua told the moon to stand, and the brook Kedron where David found the five smooth stones to fit his sling.

When they reached the brow of the last hill, however, and looked down upon Jerusalem, the past all vanished in a moment and the impor-

THE OLD GRAY WALLS OF JERUSALEM.

tant business of the hour replaced it. Again they must rely entirely upon their own resources, and there is nothing that will bring out the infinite resources of an intelligent boy like being obliged to rely upon them.

They approached the solid gray walls as few pilgrims ever came to

WAITING AT THE JAFFA GATE.

the Holy City. They saw the Tower of David, with the Turkish flag flying above it, but it meant only business to them at that moment.

It was in the gray light of early morning. There was a grand hubbub about the Jaffa gate of Jerusalem. There always is at daylight, for the caravans of merchandise constantly arriving at this commercial center of Southern Syria, usually reach their destination during the night or early in the morning, and must wait outside the gate till sunrise, when Turkish soldiers swing back the great doors.

Caravans were approaching from as far away as the eye could reach, but the boys only waited a moment to inspect the strange picture, then they entered through the needle's eye — a small door swinging in the great gate.

"'Twould be rather hard for one of those camels to get through there," Roy said as he stepped over the high sill.

"A camel without a saddle or burden of any kind can do it by trying hard," said an old man, standing inside the gate, who overheard the remark. "And so can a rich man squeeze into heaven."

ENTRANCE TO THE CHURCH OF THE HOLY SEPULCHER.

It was a bit of unexpected philosophy to find at the gate of Jerusalem, but it was philosophy, nevertheless; a profound, philosophical adjustment of analogy, at least, and Roy and Scott both turned back and looked at the needle's eye and thought it over.

After an early breakfast at the hotel, and assuring themselves that at least the captain and Louise were not stopping there, the boys started out with a guide to wander about the city.

They had only their eyes and wits to serve them, and they proposed to make the most of them.

"They reached here at least two days ago," said Roy. "If they are still here we ought to be able to find out where. They will probably go about to see something and we may meet them. If they are not here we must find out how they went away and where."

"That is the long and short of it," Scott replied.

"This is the Via Dolorosa, down which Christ carried the cross," the guide remarked in his professional monotone.

THE MOSQUE OF OMAR.

The boys glanced reverently at the Way of Pain for a moment. A city wall rose on one side and a house wall of solid stone upon the other, while far ahead a building completely arched the way. Then they continued their conversation.

The fellow went on talking as he was accustomed to. He pointed out the place where the Ecce Homo stairs had stood, and showed them the Judgment Hall, the semblance of lips in a block of granite laid in the wall, where he said one of the rocks had cried out against the injustice of the persecutors. At last they approached a small square, at the end of which stood a massive building, without form or system, rising in eccentric towers and shapeless domes. There were two great doors opening upon the court, but one of them was closed with masonry.

THE CHURCH OF THE HOLY SEPULCHER.

Here the guide grasped Scott's arm.

"The Church of the Holy Sepulcher!" he cried.

"The Church of the Holy Sepulcher," Scott repeated, rousing himself. "Let's go in."

"What a pandemonium they do keep up in there. I don't wonder

WOMEN AT THE FOUNTAIN OF BETHESDA.

the Turkish Government stations a guard of Mohammedan soldiers inside the door to prevent the Christians from fighting. The different creeds worshiping in those chapels, looked as though they would fly at one another upon the slightest provocation," Scott remarked as they came out.

"But it made a fellow feel pretty solemn going down into that vault in the natural rock, through one little chamber and into another with only those sputtering tapers for light, and to hear that priest, with his deep voice, say: 'Here sat the angels, one at the head, the other at the feet, and here the Good Lord lay.' Do you suppose it can be true?"

"This is the Mosque of Omar," said the guide, later, "erected by Omar, the second Caliph after the Prophet. It covers Mt. Moriah, and one wall rests upon one of the foundation walls of Solomon's Temple."

"Take us to the hotels and boarding houses," said Roy. And without a word the guide led the way. He could not understand them.

"Have you noticed, Roy, that there's not a wheeled vehicle in the city, nor any street wide enough for one?" Scott remarked as they continued the search; but the day ended with as little information as it began.

In the morning they heard of a veteran Jew who controlled the materials and fitted out most of the parties leaving Jerusalem for the interior. They went in search of him. He had fitted out a wealthy patron the night before, for a long journey, and had made the start with him. He would not be back till the following morning. No one else could give them any information.

"Twenty-four hours. Now's your time," Scott exclaimed, turning to

OLIVES IN THE GARDEN OF GETHSEMANE.

the guide. "What have you got that you can show us in twenty-four hours?"

"There is Bethesda, the Mount of Olives, the Garden of Gethsemane, Bethany and Bethlehem," the fellow replied.

They left the dragoman's office mounted upon three good Arab horses. They rode out of St. Stephen's Gate, passing the Pool of Bethesda, and the fountain, with the proverbial company of women about it filling earthen jugs and carrying them away balanced upon their heads.

They rode down the valley of Jehoshaphat, over the brook Kedron

and up the way that leads over the Mount of Olives, till they came to the iron gate, guarded by a Latin monk, as the entrance to the Garden of Gethsemane.

"Some of these olive-trees are more than two thousand years old, at any rate," said Roy; "and the Mount of Olives is the same, whether the garden is in the right place or not."

Then crossing the lower mound of the Mount of Olives, they rode on to Bethany.

"Do you know, Scott?" said Roy, "these things seem to grow constantly more sacred and interesting."

"I suppose the trouble is we didn't know enough to pick out what was true from all the rest at Jerusalem; but such things as Bethany are real facts," Scott replied. "Look at that old ruined tower. What a beautiful

situation.   For an Oriental city, I think Bethany is the most inviting we
have seen."

"And this is Bethlehem!" Roy said, sometime later, as they cantered
up a broad road toward an arched gate in the massive but crumbling
wall of that most favored city of all Judea.

"How closely all the houses are packed together in the Eastern
towns," he continued.   "The more vacant land there is in the neighbor-
hood the tighter they crowd their houses together, and the narrower they
make their streets."

"I know it; and up there in the North, where it is one perpetual shiver
all the year round, they seem to think that the farther they can get away

GATE OF BETHLEHEM.

from their neighbors the better.   I should think these folks would
smother packed in so tight," said Scott.

"And it's just as curious about the food," Roy added.   "You know
how they wanted everything cold up there, till they'd eat raw meat and
eat it frozen, without salt or pepper, and like it best that way.   Here
they cook everything to death.   They want it hot enough to scald a

"JEHU! HE'S A STUDY!"

fellow, and make it so fiery with red pepper and such stuff, that I am fairly raw inside."

The next morning the boys found the venerable Jew on hand.

"Jehu! but he's a study!" Scott whispered as they waited for an interview.

"He's got rather a fine look about him," Roy replied. "Of course he's dirty, but we've found precious few who were not since we left home."

A moment later he approached them, and before they could speak, he inquired in very good English:

"Have I the honor of addressing Mr. Royal Sargent and Mr. Scott Campbell?"

Their cheeks grew pale. The old dragoman must have noticed it, for without waiting for an answer, he continued: "I have a letter here for you, written by a young lady who, with her father, left for Damascus the night before last. She described you so perfectly that I knew you at once."

"To Damascus! and where from there?" Scott gasped, as Roy took the letter.

"I do not know. The gentleman purchased his outfit outright, of me, and I asked no questions. He took my best white camel; I sold the animal too cheap. I am sorry."

Without a word, Roy broke the seal and read:

I saw you this morning from my window. I tried to call, but father caught me back, and we start for Damascus to-night. Something is terribly wrong. What is it? Are you here looking for me? Is something wrong about father? If you are coming to find us, come to Damascus. I cannot escape, for father watches me all the time; but I will find some way to let you know, at Damascus, if we are there. If we go away before you come I will be sure you know where we go. Oh! I wish I knew what was the matter.   LOUISE.

Scott took the letter and read it.

" Can you fit us out for Damascus?" he asked.

" Certainly," replied the dragoman. " Horses or camels?"

" Horses, I think," said Scott, looking at Roy. " We understand them better, and this is important."

" Three horses, a dragoman, three packmules, two Arab servants. They shall be ready at sundown."

" And the price?" Scott asked.

" To hire or to purchase?" inquired the Jew.

" To purchase," Scott replied.

The bargain was made. The horses were selected. They telegraphed the *Snowbird* to go to Alexandria and return to Beyroot, as the nearest port to Damascus, and there wait for word from them.

" So," said Scott, with a deep sigh, when they sat alone in their room at the hotel, after lunch, " all is ready. It is five hours more to dinner, and an hour for that before we start. Let's turn in and have a nap."

CHAPTER XIII.

IT was two o'clock in the morning when they reached the brook Cherith, where the ravens fed Elijah, and where there still are a number of caves. A short distance beyond they passed the ruins of old Jericho, whose great walls fell to the trumpets of the hosts of Israel, and new Jericho, whose miserable mud walls have been rising and falling ever since.

The dragoman whom the Jew engaged for them was a Bedouin of the Bedouins — Raschid Airikat — a sheik of a family of sheiks dating back to the conquest. He made a very good dragoman, nevertheless, and spoke very good English.

He suggested that by a slight détour from Jericho, they could go to the Dead Sea and ride up the banks of the Jordan to the ford, where the mules and servants could go by a straight road and have everything ready for them when they arrived.

The full moon was shining as they rode down the steep hill from the plateau of Jericho and started over the desert sand for the Dead Sea, twelve miles away.

" I thought a desert was nothing but sand, but look at the clumps of low bushes every now and then. They look like sage," Roy remarked.

" They are ; desert sage shrubs," said the sheik. " In the wet season there are heavy dews upon the deserts, and the shrubs grow a little. Then they dry up and wait, as your trees do in winter."

"I thought a desert was flat," said Scott, "and here this is a perfect series of low hills, like great ocean waves."

"We are four thousand feet lower than Jerusalem and a thousand feet lower than the Mediterranean Sea," said the sheik.

"Jehu!" Scott exclaimed, "I don't wonder there's a pond at the bottom. But how does the water get out?"

"There is no outlet," replied the guide. "The Jordan pours into it, but the sun alone has to take the water out."

"I've heard that there's no living thing in those waters," Scott said, as they came to the silent sea, flashing in the moonlight. "The fish that

THE FORD OF THE JORDAN.

come down the Jordan die when they strike the sea, and some one at the hotel said that birds flying over it would drop dead."

"I reckon that's a yarn," Roy remarked; "but just look there."

All about them were fantastic forms caused by incrustations from spray blown over the rocks, with its deposit of salt and other substances.

The sheik was pointing to one of them, strongly resembling a woman, and remarked, "It is said that this is Lot's wife."

"There are lots more of them," Scott remarked. "I wonder who the rest are."

A moment more and the two boys were plunging in the dense water,

THE DEAD SEA.

trying to sink, trying to make a hand or foot stay down, while they kept bobbing up and rolling about like corks.

"A farm Down East wouldn't hire me to go into that water again," Roy exclaimed as they rode away, smarting and burning from head to foot from the effect of the Dead Sea water.

At the ford of the Jordan Roy and Scott stripped again and plunged in.

There was a caravan crossing at the time, carrying their clothes in bundles on their heads.

"We are as well dressed as they are," said Scott, "and it's simply a military necessity. In five minutes more I believe my skin would burn off."

"CITY BY THE WAY."

Their tents were pitched upon the further side, and breakfast was prepared by the time they were ready.

"This is the only possible ford for miles," remarked the sheik.

"Then of course it's where the Children of Israel crossed," said Roy, "for the Bible says it was over against Jericho."

"I wonder if this is where — what was his name, now, the general who dipped in the Jordan and cured himself of leprosy? — I never thought of that while I was in bathing.   It kind of makes me crawl," said Scott.

"Well, I washed the Dead Sea away by dipping in the Jordan, and

THE SEA OF GALILEE.

now I'm going to turn in and sleep for ten solid hours," Roy replied.

"How does it feel, Roy, waking up on the other side of Jordan?" Scott asked, as they were roused an hour before sunset.

"Feels to me as though I'd like to take another nap," Roy replied. He was ready on time, however, and they continued their journey northward, taking advantage of occasional cities and towns by the way for rest and food, or tenting when there was no other shelter at hand, passing the Sea of Galilee just as the sun was rising over the mountains, and climbing the hills toward "that opal set in emerald," the marvelous city of Damascus, lying in the incomparable valley at the confluence of the Abana and the Pharpar Rivers.

They met with a few casual adventures, with easily frightened robbers, and passed many caravans coming and going, and tribes of Arabs moving

"THE OLDEST CITY IN THE WORLD."

over the plains of Syria, but the way was too much frequented to give freedom to the wild life which the Bedouin fancies, and several times Raschid took a longer way, to avoid certain dangerous localities, though he prudently refrained from telling the boys what he was doing.

The moon was almost setting behind them as they crossed a low

PUBLIC GARDEN, DAMASCUS.

line of hills and a great gleam of white flashed in the valley before them.

" Frost ! " Scott exclaimed.

" Snow ! deep snow ! " cried Roy.

The sheik, with a grim facial contortion, which was meant for a smile, replied :

" It is the white roofs of Damascus. '

" Damascus ! " said Scott.

" Damascus ! " Roy repeated.

" It is the oldest city in the world," the sheik continued, " and the most magnificent.   When Mohammed was a young man, with his uncle's caravan he came across these hills, but here, upon the heights of Silihneh he stopped. 'Man can have but one paradise. Mine is above,' he said, and refused to go nearer to Damascus."

From the hills the white walls seemed to rise in the midst of beautiful gardens. These gardens, however, were often in inner courts completely surrounded by the homes of the wealthy, whose outer walls were as gray and dilapidated as those of Jerusalem or any other Oriental city they had visited.

It has been the prevailing custom of ages gone, and is throughout

ONE OF HER PUBLIC PLACES.

that Eastern world to-day, to beautify the interior and let the passer by see only dust and dirt and somber walls. In her public places, however, Damascus exposes even to the stranger rare glimpses of her beauty, and for ages has been known to the Persian, the Turk and the Arab as the

"THEY WERE ALWAYS CROWDED."

Pearl of the Orient. Fountains still play, and hanging gardens fill the air with perfume as they did before the time of Christ.

The streets were narrow and irregular, but the boys were becoming used to that; while the bazaars of Damascus surpassed even those of Constantinople.

Men appeared upon the streets, and merchants sat among their goods,

WEALTHY CITIZENS.

dressed in magnificent costumes, and all the rare products of the Orient appeared in the little stalls that lined the streets. There were fruits and perfumes from Arabia, spices and brilliant dyes from Babylonia; Nubia and Greece contributed their dates and grapes, Egypt and the valley of the Euphrates decorated those stalls with ostrich plumes. Darfour and the heart of the Dark Continent sent their skins and ivory. From Aleppo and India came laces, satins and muslins in wonderful handiwork. Ceylon and Linga sent from their treasures of pearls. China contributed her silks and porcelains. Turkish rugs and marvelous Bagdad carpets struggled in vain to outrival the home productions of Damascus. The Levant sent her choicest tobacco, the Moors their long-barreled matchlocks, all inlaid with mother-of-pearl, to aid the curving Damascus blade. All the wide world seemed to contribute to that bewildering bazaar. Everything useful and ornamental, that could relieve a necessity or supply a luxury to one of her citizens, could be found upon those streets. And they were always crowded. Even from sunset to sunrise people were constantly moving in the brilliant illumination of swinging lamps and burning torches.

They entered the court of an ancient temple in a secluded place

CALL TO PRAYER.

where they could yet be near the center of the city, and while preparing for a short sleep before starting upon their search through Damascus, an Arab who had followed them from outside the city, came slowly up to Scott. At first Scott thought him a beggar or a thief, and was on the

"IN THE OLD TEMPLE COURT."

point of driving him away, when he noticed that he was trying to attract his attention to a piece of brown paper which he held in his hand. At last he thrust it before his face, inquiring:

" Dis here b'long you ? "

Scott shook his head, but out of curiosity opened the paper, started, stared at it in the dim light of their camp fire, called to Roy, and the two boys, kneeling beside the fire in the old temple court, read together the brief message:

"To Bagdad, then somewhere south. Don't come. It is too far. If you do come, you shall hear from me at Bagdad, but better go home. When my father stops I will send you word. O, dear! what is the matter?"

They sent the message to the captain of the *Snowbird* at Beyroot, the seaport of Damascus, with orders to meet them or communicate at Bushire, on the Persian Gulf at the mouth of the Euphrates.

They would have started on at once, but the sheik stubbornly refused. The animals were too tired, their stores needed replenishing, and above all, the way to Bagdad was dangerous. They must wait till a caravan was starting, and join it for their own safety.

" If a caravan starts within twelve hours we will join it. If not, we shall go on alone, if we have to fight our way through the whole population of Asia," Scott exclaimed, " and you can go with us if you like, or you can go back to Jerusalem. Twelve hours from this minute, you hear me, we shall be on the road. There's the call to prayer; you can mark the time."

From a minaret not far away that musical call rang over the white walls of Damascus: " La Illaha il Allah Mahamoud Rousol il Allah ! "

Raschid bowed, turned his face toward Mecca and began his morning prayer, while Scott and Roy went into the tent and threw themselves down to sleep.

CHAPTER XIV

WHATEVER an Arab must do that he does, and when the first mugreet sounded from the minaret Raschid was ready to start for Bagdad.

There were no others going that way, but a large caravan, with an ample escort, had left Damascus the night before. They could easily overtake it, and thus insure their safety upon the long and dangerous journey over the silver-gray sand.

They rode steadily onward all night, making what was reckoned a two nights' journey as marked by caravan stages, and came upon the company early in the morning, just as it was preparing to rest for its second day. Long journeys are usually made at night, not so much because it is cooler, as because a camel will only eat by daylight. He uses his eyes to select his food instead of guiding his lips with his nose, like occidental animals, and must see what he eats or refuse it.

The caravan had spread itself over a large mountain khan, a walled inclosure about a well. They are to be found at regular intervals all of the way from Damascus to Teheran.

As the boys came down the hill toward the khan the animated picture appeared in all its inevitable fascination. There was shouting and wrangling among at least a hundred men, of many Eastern nations. Camels and dromedaries were grunting and groaning as they dropped upon their knees, then upon their haunches, in the warmest spot which

THE CARAVAN AT THE KHAN.

they could find. Some were still at the well, and some, not ready to lie
down, were quietly gazing about them, with their great, soft, dreamy
eyes, twisting their frowzy heads about on their long, curving necks.

A vulture started from the crags above, with a wild scream of dissatis-

CARAVAN ON THE MARCH.

faction. There was too much life in the picture to please his fancy, and
he flew away over the distant trail to see if any of the camels or mules
had fallen by the way. He is the great desert scavenger, and remnants
of his feasts, divided with jackals, mark every caravan trail that crosses a
desert, in skeletons growing whiter and whiter in the sun.

When a camel lay down the owner fastened him by tying a cord
about his folded leg, so that he could not straighten it, and when the
day's rest was over he brought the creature slowly to his feet again by a
series of jerks upon the halter and punches on the shoulder. During
each operation the camel grunted and groaned as though his very life
was departing.

The path followed the general course of the Euphrates River for a
time. and here and there between them and the river stretched broad

plains covered with grain. It was planted by Bedouin tribes where pos-
sibilities of irrigation gave them an opportunity to subdue the desert
sand. All through the grain fields perches were erected upon four poles
thrust into the ground. On each of these perches sat two or three
naked little Arabs, with piles of stones beside them and slings in their
hands, to keep the birds away.

"Good shot!" cried Scott, as they watched a little fellow use his
sling. "He killed that bird on the wing, more than fifty feet away."

"I shouldn't wonder if King David got his skill in practicing at some
such business as this," said Roy. "I've seen ever so many things in the
last two weeks that are just like Bible stories. I don't believe these parts
have changed very much in the last two thousand years."

For their own convenience and to avoid the attention they would
otherwise attract, the boys had purchased native clothes and pronounced
them vastly more comfortable than American costumes. The *abba*, a
large white cloak, hung so loose about them that the sunlight had little
effect. There was nothing to cramp them during a long night in the
saddle, and the *effie*, like a huge napkin bound upon their heads, was very
much more convenient than a hat. It was a curious sensation, however,

A CAMEL FASTENED

and Scott declared that he became accustomed to seeing Roy dressed
like a heathen much quicker than he did to finding himself sailing under
the same rigging.

"It isn't much like walking the deck, and I don't think I should like to do it for a living," Roy said one day as they rode along a little in advance of the caravan, to escape the dust; for they were again upon the unbroken sand and "out of sight of land," as they termed the green fields and an occasional oasis.

"Well, it's better than catching cod, any way," Scott replied. "But what's that — a thunder storm coming up?"

"Rain on a desert!" Roy exclaimed, "rain on a desert! whoever

AFTER THE BIRDS.

heard of such a thing? They didn't tell us to bring umbrellas."

"But it is a thunder cloud, and a big one," Scott insisted.

Just then Raschid came riding up.

"Looks like rain," Scott remarked.

"It will rain, and in five minutes," replied the sheik in great excitement. "It will rain sand! Cover your faces, and don't for anything get it in your eyes or throats."

He set the example, but Scott opened his mouth for one more inquiry, when a sharp gust of wind struck him and instantly his mouth was filled with gritty sand as fine as emery. He decided not to ask the question.

The horses began to shiver and tremble, and huddle together. Ras-

SAND STORM IN THE DESERT.

chid took the front, with another Arab who had accompanied him. Scott dismounted and crouched behind his horse, while Roy turned his back upon the hurricane as far as he could, by bending down over his horse's neck.

In the caravan just behind them, the camels all lay down, twisting their heads round between their legs and shutting their nostrils so tight that one could hardly have found them. The men too lay down under shelter of the camels.

The storm was not long, though severe, but as they rode on, with cracked lips and bloodshot eyes, Raschid told them of sand storms through which he had passed when men and camels were completely buried before the sand ceased drifting.

RASCHID AIRIKAT AT REST.

At last they camped in a beautiful oasis only one night's journey from Bagdad.

Toward the end of a long journey camels move very slowly. They did not reach this oasis till nearly noon. The next stage also was a long one, and the leader of the caravan announced that they should not leave the place till the afternoon of the following day. The boys were determined to go on, but Raschid explained to them that the last stage before Bagdad was particularly dangerous from robbers, and that beside the trouble they would surely receive if they met with wandering tribes, there was an unwritten chivalry of the desert which compelled one who had enjoyed the

THE WANDERER.

protection of a caravan to render service in return and remain under command of the leader to the end. Reluctantly, they remained. They were not sorry, however, for during the early evening they made their first attempt at camel riding. Raschid borrowed three camels from a friend whose acquaintance he had made, and he and the boys started round the oasis, much to the amusement of the Arabs.

A camel steps forward with both feet on one side, then with both feet on the other side, swinging back and forth like a ship at sea, and as he moves forward with each step the fellow seated upon the hump continually describes a complete circle.

Raschid Airikat sat upon his camel, leisurely smoking while it ran, as much at rest as though he had been rocking in a cradle, but Scott and Roy, the moment they found themselves whirling, sure that they were about to fly off in one direction or another, clutched the saddle as they would a life rope in a storm.

"That's the worst ship I've been aboard of yet," Scott gasped, as the camels returned and with many a grunt and groan lay down, for the riders to dismount.

"It's funny how they steer with just one rein, like the Lapps," said Roy. "And have you noticed that many of the Arabs have only one rein for their horses, too?"

"They guide the horses with their knees," remarked the sheik. "Press upon one side and an Arab horse will always turn to the other. We use our hands for fighting, not for holding reins."

As Scott and Roy sat upon the edge of the oasis that night, looking at a camel that had wandered off over the sand, an Arab approached, watching them closely and looking cautiously about in every direction. Seeming satisfied at last, and sitting down close to them, he said:

"THE CARAVAN STARTED AGAIN."

"Two people from far across sea, in great danger, but not know."

"Danger!" Scott repeated, lifting his eyebrows a little, for he was too bold and inexperienced to realize the full import of the word. "Sand storms are tough, but not dangerous."

"I speak of storm that sweeps the breath away," replied the Arab. "Out of Damascus there passed a wind one day, with a sunbeam in its breast. The wind is sharp and keen. The sunbeam soft and beautiful.

"GLOOMY, DINGY, DIRTY."

Into the Arab's ear the wind whisper: 'In the Khan by ruined temple are two from far over sea. If they follow where I go Arab follow too. Send them away upon the long journey. Bring me word at Bagdad, with good proof, and have a piece of gold for every finger on Arab's hands.' Then into Arab's eyes the sunbeam shone and shook her head. Day and night I follow, from Damascus to Bagdad. I think of ten gold pieces and lift the knife. I think of the sunbeam and it falls again. Now I tell for strangers go Bagdad and wind may whisper in another ear when Sunbeam cannot shake her head. God is God. There is but one God, and Mohammed is his Prophet. Whatever of good betideth cometh from Him. Whatever of evil is thine own doing. God go with you."

With that blessing from the Koran the Mohammedan rose to leave.

"Stop a bit," said Scott. "He wanted you to kill us, did he?"

The Arab bowed his head.

"You would be willing to do it for ten gold pieces?"

Again he bowed.

"It's quite a loss to you, then, to give it up, isn't it?"

"The smile of the sunbeam is greater gain," replied the Arab.

"There's your money," said Scott, handing him ten English sovereigns, "and the sun will shine for you beside. Now will you answer a question, honestly?"

"By the beard of the Prophet, if I lie may my bones whiten in this sand," he replied.

"Are you going to meet them in Bagdad?"

The Arab shook his head.

"Why not?"

"I could not prove that I had sent the strangers upon the long journey. I should receive no money, but a curse."

"You know where to find them?"

The Arab bowed.

"Well, here's an idea for you, you old rascal. Here's my watch. He'll know it, for he gave it to me for pulling him out of the water once. Roy, give him that handkerchief with your name on it. There! kill a cat if you can find one, and sprinkle them with blood. Let him think our bones are bleaching on the sand if it will please him; I don't care; and if he pays you ten gold pieces more, why, so much the better for you. Only carry a letter for us to the sunbeam and bring us an answer, and you shall have still another reward; see?"

The Arab bowed his head, and Scott and Roy, with a black crayon, on a strip of white cloth, wrote to Louise that they were still alive, were following close behind and should keep on following; that there was something very wrong, but nothing they could do to set it right except to follow on wherever her father went; that they proposed to follow him to the end of the world, but that no harm should come to any one; and that sometime they should find an opportunity to see her and tell her all about it.

The Arab took the cloth, folded it carefully and put it in his turban, saying:

"I will bring answer to the coffee house just outside the river gate of Old Bagdad, upon the other bank of the Tigris." With that he disappeared.

The caravan started again late the next day, and in the gray light of early morning entered the Damascus gate of the gloomy, dingy, dirty city of Bagdad. From the distance it had seemed one vast jungle of beautiful green, but all the foliage was in the hidden courts. The streets were narrower than the narrowest the boys had seen. The walls were gloomier than the gloomiest. Not a single window was visible anywhere. Even the doors were narrow and low. No sun ever touched the pavement anywhere.

As they entered the gate a man took his place in front and walked before the lead camel, shouting:

"*Am Amahl Rhue!*" at the top of his lungs, warning people to turn down some side street, out of the way of the caravan, for it was impossible for two camels to pass in many of those narrow streets.

"Only look at those creatures," Scott exclaimed as they passed a little open square, less than fifteen feet in width.

"Poor wretches!" Roy replied, "living human beings, mortals! immortals, I suppose; why, they are hardly brutes, wallowing in that filth."

"There's an old friend, any way," Scott added as they passed a side street at the corner of which stood a beggar, extending a lank and dirty hand in a mute appeal for charity.

"They seem to know how to beg most everywhere. Upon my word, I thought at first the fellow wanted to shake hands with us," Roy replied.

"Did you mind the baby, though!" cried Scott, "the little youngster clinging to his head, with his eyes all covered with flies? He didn't seem to mind 'em much, but if I'd had a bottle of Col. Sellers' Ointment I'd given him a dose. Bet he'd felt better afterward, even if he didn't know enough to be bothered by them before."

"And there's another familiar thing I see," said Roy.

"Jehu! a water-carrier!" Scott exclaimed. "Jerusalem! but what a face. Roy Sargent, did you ever see the like? Just think of that fellow rigged up in fur and set down among the grinning Lapps. I should think he'd turn the water in that jug into lemonade without sugar!"

"Lemonade!" Roy gasped. "O, Scott! why did you mention that? I'd almost walk from here to Damascus for a glass of Aunt Betsey's lemonade."

Here and there a mosque, with its slender minaret, claimed a little open space, and at last the caravan entered the great Khan, and the clamor and hubbub of unpacking began. The boys were not anxious to remain longer with the caravan. They had seen enough of camels and Arabs, and were anxious to reach the coffee shop.

They simply crossed the Khan, with its open mosque, among whose

"ANOTHER FAMILIAR THING."

pillars some people from the caravan were already offering thanks for their safe journey, and beggars were in appropriate positions to receive thank offerings from such as felt disposed.

" Bagdad is the home of the great caliphs, full of all the mysteries of the East," remarked Raschid as they emerged from the narrow streets upon the broad Tigris, rushing between the two cities, Old and New Bagdad, and rode out upon a bridge of boats, rising and falling and trembling upon the waves rushing under it.

" The embankment upon that side of the river was laid by Nebuchad-

INTERIOR OF KHAN.

nezzar, King of Babylon," Raschid continued, "and the new city upon this side, was built by my great ancestor Haroun el Raschid and his beautiful queen Zobeide."

" And it was here that the foundation for the Arabian Nights was borrowed, I believe," Roy remarked as they entered Old Bagdad, not so old or dilapidated or gloomy, after all, as New Bagdad, many centuries younger.

" You should see the interiors of some of the gorgeous homes behind these walls if you would behold in reality even greater magnificence than is pictured in those tales," Raschid remarked.

AT THE LETTER-WRITER'S BOOTH.

It seemed so impossible to believe that Roy and Scott set it down as simply a patriotic romance on the part of their guide, glorifying the relic of his ancestors. Indeed, there may have been a little exaggeration in the sheik's estimate, yet it is quite true that the homes of Bagdad are as

IN THE MOSQUE.

marvelously beautiful and mysterious in their interiors as they are gloomy and plain externally.

Old Bagdad, however, was more open, and booths appeared in the broader streets where, in New Bagdad, they were all crowded into narrow market places. In a little ornamented stall a foreign letter-writer sat at work, with his brush and ink-pot, writing a letter. Before him on his gorgeous rug sat one of the pretty belles of Bagdad, looking as though she had come, bodily, from the famous old romance. Beside her sat a black slave, her nurse; and in the momentary glimpse which the boys obtained, it was quite evident that the nurse was dictating the letter while the pretty, pale-faced belle sat smiling and nodding her approval to the foreign scribe.

"Wonder how our girls at home would like it if that was the only way that they could read and write," said Scott.

" I don't know how they would like it," Roy replied. " but I know that I shouldn't like it much."

" Look at their shoes standing there on the sill," Scott exclaimed. " They're almost as bad as stilts. I don't wonder they take them off before they try to sit down."

" Well, I don't wonder they put them on when they go to walk," Roy replied. " For my part, I should want stilts in good earnest if I was to go far on foot in these filthy streets."

Then they passed through the river gate and out upon the broad valley stretching down the banks of the Tigris, through a vast collection of ruins — mosques, palaces and tombs — each with its story of the grand days of centuries ago: but the most attractive sight to them was the coffee house, where they secured a room, with Bagdad rugs for beds, and

BAGDAD FROM THE RIVER.

Bagdad rugs for chairs, and one little window looking out over the Tigris.

" I tell you, I should like to strike a sofa somewhere, or a lounge, and I should like to sleep again in a Christian bed, if it was no better than a bunk on the *Snowbird*," said Roy.

"Well, so should I, when the time comes," Scott replied; "but under the circumstances, this is good enough for me;" and like an Oriental born and bred he stretched himself upon the mat, with his arm for a

THE COFFEE HOUSE.

pillow, and with the *effie* pulled down over his face was fast asleep in five minutes.

As the sun was sinking toward the west the boys sat watching the brilliant glow upon the river and the lights and shadows over the curiously tinted bricks of which the walls of New Bagdad are built, when the

Arab of the oasis suddenly appeared and handed them a letter. It was hastily written. It simply said:

"Father saw you, this morning, at the Khan. We are going by steamer to day — South somewhere; Ceylon, I think. Take care. My father wants to kill you. Go home, and when he stops wandering I will tell you where we are."

It was not even signed.

"Did you get your money from him?" Scott asked.

"Yes; last night, and gave the letter. This morning I go for answer. He try kill me. He see you live. I run. I wait. I watch. Sunbeam drop the letter out of palanquin when it pass me by the wharf."

"Has the steamer gone?" Roy gasped.

"An hour ago," replied the Arab.

"What does it matter, Roy?" Scott asked. "We could not touch him here, and he would have us killed in spite of all that we could do to keep track of ourselves. He's desperate. For my part, I'd much rather he'd show the coward that's in him by running in this way. By and by we shall corner him somewhere where his wind will fail, and he'll have to lay to. I'm glad he's left this country, any way."

"When does the next steamer sail?" asked Roy.

"One week," replied the Arab.

Roy and Scott looked at each other aghast.

"That's more than I bargained for," said Scott.

"Me, too," said Roy, "and by a very large majority."

A MOHAMMEDAN MOSQUE.

They paid the Arab and sent him away. Then they summoned Raschid and directed him to procure for them the fastest craft of any kind to be found upon the river. He had already sold their horses and mules in the market place for almost as much as they had paid for them in Jerusalem.

Raschid had learned to obey, and obey quickly; a difficult lesson for an Arab; and in less than an hour there lay in the river just below the coffee house, as marvelous a craft as ever Yankee sailor stepped upon. It was the orthodox Euphrates boat, however, and no better, no worse — except in age — could have been procured for them.

"How did you get it?" Scott asked.

"I bought it for the price of the two mules," said Raschid. "And there was enough besides to pay for fruit and food, which you will find in the cabin."

"Where are the men to run her?" Roy inquired.

"There are none," said Raschid. "The boatmen of Bagdad will not move upon the river after dark."

"We'll run her ourselves, then!" Scott exclaimed. "Will you and the mule drivers go with us to help out?"

"We have contracted to follow you, young gentlemen, till you send us back," the sheik replied good-naturedly.

"A MARVELOUS CRAFT."

"Then hurry the luggage aboard, just as it came from the mules, and push off. We'll find out how to manage her when we're afloat," said Roy, and in ten minutes they were moving with the current away from Bagdad, toward the Euphrates and the Persian Gulf.

What little wind there was blew well for them, and as the sun touched the horizon they succeeded in lifting the second sail.

"You can't just call it hoisting," Scott remarked; "but they're there, all the same."

"And likely to stay there," Roy added; "for I believe it would beat an admiral to get them down again. Hope we don't have any squalls."

"By the way, Captain," Scott exclaimed, "how do you like going to sea again? I can't touch my hat to you, now, but I'll pull down the point of my *effie*, if that will do you any good."

"What a world of wonders!" Roy replied. "Suppose, when we were hauling codlines on the Banks last spring, some one had told us that in less than eight months we should be rigged out like born Arabs, sole owners and officers of a scow like this on the Tigris River?"

" Look at how dark it is!" Scott exclaimed, suddenly turning about as he held the bar which moved the rudder. " Five minutes ago the sun was shining, and now I can hardly see the prow. The sun makes dreadful easy work of going down in these parts."

For their first night "at sea" the boys were afraid to trust either lookout or helm out of their own hands, and they took turns, relieving each other by changing places occasionally as they moved swiftly down the river, with a strong current and a good breeze.

" Roy," Scott called, " starboard a little and run in toward shore. What are those dark objects moving round there on the bank?"

" Don't know." Roy replied. " If they're natives we don't want to get too close to them at this time of night."

" Wish I had the *Snowbird's* night glass," Scott muttered. " They're

DARK OBJECTS ON THE BANK.

doing something, whoever they are, and there's lots of them. I'm going to call Raschid."

The sheik was quickly on his feet. They were near the shore now, and looking for a moment, he muttered :

" Crocodiles," and shrugged his shoulders.

" Guess we'd better keep in deep water," Roy remarked, putting back the helm.

As morning dawned they passed a small stream flowing into the Tigris.

" Look up there, will you, Scott?" Roy cried, as he stood in his turn in the prow. " For mercy's sake! It's a grand convention of long-legged storks. flamingoes or something."

" That must be where they all come from," Scott replied.

" Or where they all go to," Roy added. " I wonder the crocodiles don't go up there hunting."

"I should desperately like to take a bath," Scott remarked as Raschid took his position at the prow, and one of the mule drivers, who had been a boatman in his day, relieved Roy at the helm, while the other was cooking their breakfast.

"Me, too," Roy replied, "but I'm nct over anxious to find myself inside the shell of one of those crocodiles, so I guess I'll eat something and take a nap."

The sheik called them before their sleep had half-satisfied them, to see two large ostriches that were close upon the river bank.

"They are some of my people," said Raschid. "Egypt claims them as her own, and has many more of them than Arabia; but the finest birds in the world and the most beautiful plumage can be found upon the borders of our desert."

"I didn't know that we were near Arabia," Scott exclaimed. "Why, we seem to have traveled ten thousand miles in the last three weeks, but we were close to Arabia when we started."

"We have been skirting the borders of Arabia ever since we left Jerusalem," replied Raschid. "And sometimes we have been quite near. Now we are not far from the ancient city of Bashra, upon the great caravan trail from Mecca to Babylon and Persia."

The boys drew a long breath. They could not even yet realize that it was not at least partly a dream. It did not seem possible that they

"A GRAND CONVENTION."

were really in the midst of these landmarks of the very oldest civilization known to history.

"What are those people doing over there?" Scott called, from the prow to Roy, who held the helm, the following day.

Roy looked across the plain through which they were passing.

There were low, flat huts in sight, as white as the driven snow, and through fields of grain natives were running, frantically waving something, while all about them clouds of dust seemed drifting in the air.

"I know," Scott exclaimed a moment later. "They're locusts, eating the grain, and those folks are after them. See! the air is full of them, all about us. O, Roy! just look at that cloud of them."

A moment later they had no need to look far, for the deck, the masts, the sails, were covered with them, and every one had to lend a hand to drive them off, before they found the food and got into the cabin.

Then birds came sailing through the cloud enjoying a grand feast.

"I say, Scott," Roy remarked, "between those kytes and crows I'll bet on the kytes. Do you see, a kyte catches a locust in his claw and goes right on flying while he eats, so as to be on hand for another bite the minute one is down, while the crows catch them in their beaks and have to go sit down on a branch to eat."

They were anxious to see the ancient city of Bassorah, but there was a good breeze and a strong current behind them and they decided not to

RASCHID'S COUNTRYMEN.

stop. Raschid told them many wonderful tales of the old days of the conquest, when Kahled the Invincible led his victorious Mohammedan armies into Persia from this point, and of that Bedouin boy, Kanana, who, mounted upon a black dromedary, brought a message from the . Caliph Omar at Mecca to Kahled at Bashra, in thirteen days, when no one had ever made the journey before in less than three weeks.

All they saw of Bashra, however, was a Bedouin boy sitting cross-legged on a stone abutment upon the river bank.

They sailed from the Tigris into the Euphrates and then over the Persian Gulf, dodging among the pearl dhows filling the beautiful Bay of Linga.

One after another the divers would draw up a heavy block of hermatite, attached to a rope, and catching it in their hands let themselves rapidly down to the famous oyster beds where they would quickly fill the small wire baskets which hung at their waists. They remained under water not over one minute, when they were pulled up, emptied the contents of their baskets upon the deck, for others to sort and open, and threw themselves down to lie in the sun and pant. The water was so clear that they could easily see them working, twenty feet below.

Beyond them lay the town of Bushire, with its almond orchards and orange groves.

They found the Parsee overseer of the pearl fisheries at Bushire already expecting them. He had received communications from the

"THEY'RE LOCUSTS, EATING THE GRAIN."

Snowbird concerning them, and a message for them from the captain, which said :

"The treasure is all at Ceylon. We shall reach there as soon as possible, and remain unless the luggage is removed. If so we shall leave word for you. Send any orders there."

To this they replied :

"We shall reach Ceylon by steamer from Bushire in ten days or less. Capt. D. is one week ahead. Follow luggage."

They found the Parsee a most amiable man, very proud of a few
European notions he had introduced into his home—chairs and tables
among the rest—and very ready to aid them in disposing of their lumber-
ing craft and Oriental belongings which were of no further use to them,

as well as providing themselves with necessities for a steamer trip.

"Will those oyster fields never fail?" Roy asked, as they sat on the
veranda that evening, fanned by a punka and looking over the bay.

"I think not," replied their host. "Century after century has seen
the divers working in the Gulf of Linga. Babylon and Nineveh were
supplied by them. Solomon and the Queen of Sheba counted their
wealth in these products. Pompeii and Herculaneum were rich with
them. Damascus and Egypt gloried in them. Persia and Greece
adorned themselves with countless wealth and beauty from beneath these
waves, and the greater the world became the greater demand only re-
sulted in more dhows, more divers and more pearls. Last year the first
cost of the pearls, exported, amounted to more than three million dollars.
This year they have taken more than last, and a thousand years to come
I fancy it will be just the same."

A steamer stopped at Bushire early in the morning, and the boys
were once more under way, having arranged for their escort to return to

GAMES ON DECK.

Jerusalem. The hours passed rapidly enough with a merry company and new mode of travel. There were always games going on among the passengers on deck, and almost before they knew it they were dropping anchor in the beautiful, landlocked harbor of Point de Galle, at the southern extremity of the large island of Ceylon.

The little town at the head of the harbor was almost buried in foliage. Palms of all sorts crowded each other to the very water's edge wherever one might turn. A dense tropical jungle rose like a beautiful wall about them, brilliant with enormous flowers, laden with fruit and knitted together with trailing vines, twisting and twining and hanging in deep festoons over the water.

It was so different from anything they had seen before that the boys stood watching and admiring, almost forgetting to look for the *Snowbird*.

"Look at those sail-boats!" Scott exclaimed. "The boat is only an immense canoe, too narrow for two to sit down side by side and it rises three feet out of the water."

"Look at the amount of sail they carry!" Roy added. "That's an idea, now. See those two horns curving way out over the water on the port side? See that sharpened log at the end? That's what does the business. They can sit on the rail and be high out of the water, and a hurricane couldn't capsize them."

THE BEAUTIFUL COAST.

Before the boys realized it the deck was crowded with natives; guides, servants and hotel clerks, clamoring for patrons, and salesmen with everything Ceylon produced, so eager to sell that they bid against themselves, lower and lower, coming down from their first price till one would think they must surely offer to give away their goods before they had done with a customer, if he refused to purchase.

There was fruit — no end of it — and precious stones without limit. There were brilliant birds in bamboo cages, eating green sugar cane, and everything imaginable made of shell and fancy woods.

The boys were much more interested, however, in a letter from the captain of the *Snowbird*, saying:

"We lay at anchor two days at Point de Galle. Received your message. Capt. D. and daughter arrived. They took the treasure on board same steamer and sailed at once for Singapore. We follow. Shall wait you there or leave word."

Point de Galle is the great transfer center for all Oriental steamers. Roy and Scott left the steamer at once, without even going on shore, and were taken on board another sailing at once for China, by way of the Malay Peninsula.

Early one morning they were roused by the stopping of the steamer's wheels, and a moment later were summoned on deck. There they found the *Snowbird* lying at close quarters, and were not long in transferring themselves and their luggage to her deck, where a hearty welcome awaited them.

"We didn't want you to land from the steamer," said the captain, "for our man has spies at Singapore and Penang, on the lookout for you. He has gone into the interior as the guest of an ivory trader who has a large bungalow there. He shipped the treasure to Australia, but met the trader on the steamer, and is to stay a month or two with him, hunting elephants. He is in the kingdom

THE PARSEE OVERSEER.

of Siam, and the king is a very sensible sovereign. We shall have no trouble in securing his permission to arrest Captain Downing, but to obtain it we must run to Bangkok, the capital. Then we can make short work by crossing the peninsula from the other side, where he is not expecting us."

So they rounded the southern point of Malacca, with Sumatra, then

THE DECK WAS CROWDED WITH NATIVES.

Borneo, upon the starboard, and sailed up the China Sea and into the Gulf of Siam.

"All I ever heard about Siam was Siamese twins," said Scott. "I don't suppose they're all twins there, are they?"

The captain laughed heartily and assured the boys that they would be surprised in more ways than one when they reached the capital of Siam.

CHAPTER XV.

AT THE END OF THE POLE.

"DO you notice that we cast no shadow," Roy said, as Scott stood beside him at the helm. "Look! when I stand up straight the shadow of my cap just covers my feet."

"It's not much like the first of our running the *Snowbird*," Scott replied. "where our shadows were half a mile long most of the time. And what a blessing it is to have regular winds that you can depend upon, blowing steadily in one direction for six solid months, instead of those gales and hurricanes from all directions at once, and without enough of warning to take in sail. But what in the name of wonder is that thing coming between those islands. I say, Captain," he called, "what sort of a craft is that?"

"She's a Chinese trading junk when she's at a good distance," the captain muttered, "but give her a wide berth. She'll be a pirate if she comes too close."

"A pirate!" Roy exclaimed.

"Who cares?" said Scott. "We could outrun her three miles to two."

"Don't be too sure," replied the captain. "Those sails are more scientific than ours, even if they don't look so well. They can make the most of every breath of wind, and that junk will stand a deal of straining. Better keep well to port." He was frowning as he stood watching the craft coming between the islands.

" We've an old rusty cannon in the fo'castle," Roy remarked, intending it for a joke, but at that moment the junk put her nose several points about and, turning sharply, the captain ordered in quick succession:

"Heave out that cannon, boys, quicker than lightning! All hands to it! Run her for'ard on the port bow! Swing open the water-gate. Quick! Run her nose through as far as you can. Open the aft water-gate. Swing round enough to show 'em a full broadside," he added, turning to Roy, then, back again to the crew, where Scott and the Russian official were working with the cook and the seamen. "Run up the colors! Be lively! Now stand by, every man of you to the port rail," and in the twinkling of an eye every order was obeyed. If the boys had doubted the necessity at first they saw the value of experience and energy before they came to the end.

"A PIRATE."

The junk had headed for them and was bearing down, with at least fifty ugly-looking, half-naked seamen huddled in the prow. As the water gate swung open, disclosing the cannon's mouth, the flag shot up and unfurled, and eight stalwart fellows appeared along the port rail; there was a yell from the junk, and over the water came a distant cry:

"No shootee! No shootee! Mellikan man all litee!" and the junk put about again and went on her way.

The boys laughed heartily when all was over, and Scott exclaimed, "We haven't a single shot in the locker to fit that gun."

"That is of no consequence," replied the captain. "It is eternal vigilance, and not a locker full of cannon balls, that is the price of safety."

Their first surprise upon entering the harbor of Bangkok, was to pass a well-built hut drifting slowly down the bay.

" It has only broken from its moorings," said the captain, and a little later they discovered whole streets laid out in the water, as regularly as upon the shore, with shops and booths and markets.   Behind them rose the city itself, sheltered by mountains, with beautiful porcelain towers and a modern fort, above which floated a red flag with a white elephant. *

This was Bangkok, the capital of Siam.

The first sight to greet them as they went on shore was a company of Malay sailors sitting upon the ground, eating an open-air lunch with chopsticks.

"And look at that barber!" Roy exclaimed.   "He's everlastingly like a Chinaman, and dressing a lady's hair, right out in the street."

"A horse car, or I'm an Esquimau!" Scott cried a moment later, as a jingling bell attracted their attention.

"And electric lights!" Roy added.   "Scott, is this Siam or civilization?"

" I reckon it's a little of both," Scott replied.   " The fact is, Roy, I'm

"BROKEN FROM ITS MOORINGS."

getting so used to being surprised that I wonder how I ever got on at the humdrum of codfishing."

Through the American minister the boys easily obtained a permit to place their request before the Siamese authorities and were summoned to the palace, for that purpose. They were ushered into a room where a young man in half-European dress sat upon a sofa surrounded by three little Siamese boys.

He was evidently some secretary of the court, for he at once began to

THE CROWN PRINCE'S PALACE.

talk to them about their business. They were reluctant, at first, to tell him their story, as they hoped for an interview with some high official; but he spoke excellent English, and as no one else appeared they gradually told him all, showing him their papers from the Russian Government.

When they had finished he said that the crown prince was to hold a reception that night, in the course of his majority festival, and that if they would leave the papers with him till then, and would honor the crown prince by attending, with the two Russians, he would see that they then received their answer.

"Do you suppose the fellow had any right to ask us?" Scott inquired when they returned to the *Snowbird*.

"Doubtless he had," replied the captain, "and I am very sure that we had better accept. Until a boy is fourteen, in Siam, his hair, on the top of his head, is kept carefully done up in a little pug. Then it is cut off and he becomes a man. With the crown prince there is always a great festival at the same time, and you will see a deal that you'll never have a chance to see again."

Much against their inclinations the sailor boys made the most of their wardrobes to fit themselves for the occasion and joined the bewildering throng of magnificently dressed nobles, doing honor to the little fourteen-year-old crown prince of Siam, who sat in an upholstered and richly

IT WAS THE KING.

ornamented throne, and surrounded by an array of marvelous gifts.

"Jehu! Roy, just look at that fellow over on the right, all silk and lace and diamonds," Scott whispered.

"He wears the signet," said the Russian officer. "He is the king."

Scott turned upon him with a face full of blank astonishment and replied :

"He's the very fellow we talked with this morning."

A few minutes later he came to welcome them. He said that he had directed that the papers be returned to the *Snowbird*, with proper authority from Siam to make the arrest desired.

"You say that you propose to cross the mountains from Rajok," he added. " I am sorry that I can not offer you elephants for the journey, but my elephants are never at Rajok till the hunting season. There is a good, smooth road, however. Do you ride the bicycle ? "

Scott managed to shake himself out of his astonishment enough to reply:

"Of course we do, sir."

The king only smiled at the absence of court etiquette in the bewildered sailor-boy, and continued: " The wheel is my favorite. From Rajok you can reach the trader's bungalow in one day. I have done it myself. It is a fine place. He is a friend of mine. I will have four wheels sent to your vessel to-night. When you have done with them you can leave them with the Governor of Rajok. I wish you success."

"Of all things under heaven !" Scott exclaimed, as

THROUGH THE JUNGLE.

they began the journey a few days later, leaving the *Snowbird* anchored in the harbor of Rajok. "We have driven the dogs in their sledges in Greenland, the reindeer in their poulkas in Lapland, the cobs in carjols in Norway, three horses abreast in a hayrick in Russia, and camels on the Syrian desert, but whoever thought of riding in a horse car in Bangkok or crossing Siam on a bicycle. Down breaks! Jehu! what's that?"

"It's nothing much, and yet it may be serious," replied the captain as

CROSSING THE STREAM.

he rode in advance. "Come on! There's nothing for it but to bolt," and swinging one hand he made a dash, followed by the officer and Scott and Roy in line.

A black-buck bull had taken possession of the path, where a steep hill rose on one side and a steeper precipice fell away on the other.

For a moment there was a decided uncertainty, but the black-buck was the most bewildered of the whole. He bellowed and lashed the rock with his tail till the last moment, then he whirled about and ran.

At the bungalow they learned that the trader and his guest, with the young lady and most of the servants, were off upon an elephant hunt, and leaving their wheels they started on foot, guided by a Malay, for a walk of ten miles and more, through the dense tropical jungles to where the tents of the party were pitched.

They were all well armed, but the officer, who now took command of the party, warned them not to use a weapon unless in self-defense, until he gave the order.

"DOWN BREAKS! JEHU! WHAT'S THAT?"

"What a wonderful place a tropical jungle is," Roy exclaimed. "Scott, could you ever tell anybody about this place so that they could understand?"

Chattering monkeys, screaming birds and animals were everywhere,

"I WOULDN'T DISTURB THEM."

and the jungle grew denser and denser till, at times, it was almost impossible for them to make their way, even under the skillful guidance of the stalwart Malay.

"Look at those hanging vines!" said Roy, "and at those enormous ferns. Glory! see those flowers. They are almost large enough for easy-chairs."

"What?" cried Scott. "Are we expected to undress to wade across that little stream? Bet a cent I can jump it. It's not up to my knees."

"THEIR FIRST ELEPHANTS."

"The guide is taking off his clothes," replied the captain, "and he knows the place better than we do."

Scott said no more, for a moment later the Malay was up to his neck in water that was so clear that the bottom did not seem twelve inches from the surface.

"What's that?" Roy gasped, as they started on again. "A man, crouching along the ground!"

"And another swinging from the trees!" Scott added, clutching his rifle. "Jehu! look at his eyes!"

"I wouldn't disturb them if I were you," said the captain. "I have met those fellows before. They are orang-outangs. The Malay word for man is orang, and outang means 'of the woods.' That thing crouching along is a mother. See her little one clinging to her, between her arms. They're timid creatures, and they'll not disturb us if we let them rest, but that father, swinging there, has more strength in one of his arms than twenty men."

" As we're on other business I suppose we'll have to touch our caps to him," Scott replied, dropping his rifle, " but upon my word I hate to see a fellow make up a face like that at me and not assert my dignity."

Now the forest grew more open again. The trees were larger and taller, and soon they heard a boisterous splashing and shrill screaming, as they came out upon the bank of a river of considerable size, where they discovered elephants bathing and dashing water over each other, while one, upon the bank, was tearing a vine from a tree and eating it.

The guide shook his head, to indicate that the hunting party was not there, and made a wide détour about the elephants.

Presently, however, another sound caught his watchful ear. He

" TWO GLEAMING TUSKS TRANSFIXED HIM."

made a sharp exclamation, pointed to a tree and set the example by climbing it.

The four readily took the hint, but were hardly among the branches when a huge dusky figure came plunging into view, following close upon several human beings who were running for their lives.

It was an enormous tusker elephant, and from those whom he pursued he seemed to single out two white men, running side by side.

"Captain Downing!" Scott exclaimed.

"Captain Downing!" Roy repeated.

They were coming nearer. They were making for a large tree, with its gnarled roots thrust into the air about its base, not twenty feet from where the boys had taken refuge.

The angry elephant was close upon them. At the last moment the trader, skilled in hunting the elephant, made a dart to one side and sprang behind the tree. It was an old trick. The elephant could not get about that huge trunk so rapidly as the man, and while he was trying to reach him the Malay servants would find their chance to attack him.

Captain Downing, less expert, attempted to do the same thing, tripped up on one of the roots, fell upon his face, his rifle flying from his grasp, and before he c'' move two gleaming tusks trans .. im. The infuriated animal, on his bended knees, pushed ha 'er and harder, throwing th' w ' f his enormous head upon the body of his victim.

In one moment the life would be crushed out of him. Scott dropped from the branch upon which he was sitting. Roy, the Russians and the

THE CAPTAIN MEETS LOUISE.

Malay shouted to him to come back, but he did not heed them. He caught the rifle from where it fell, threw it to his shoulder, aimed for the elephant's eye and in an instant sent a ball crashing into the creature's brain. The rest gathered courage from the example, and before the elephant could extricate himself three more bullets pierced him and he fell dead.

They dragged the mangled body of Captain Downing to one side. He was still living. His eyes rested on Scott and Roy and he recognized them instantly. The sight seemed to trouble him, and having no desire to make his dying moments bitter they walked away, leaving him with the Russians, to whom he made a clean confession, saying that he had also deceived his daughter, telling her that she was not his child, but that he had adopted her in infancy and that she was the real heiress. His last words were thanks that he had lived long enough to make the confession, and there, in the Malay forest, Captain Downing died, and his poor mangled body was buried under the same tree where the accident occurred.

Guided by two Malays the " an officer went alone to the camp to break the sad news to Louise.

The had set and the moon was shining over the jungle as he approached the tent.

He paused outside and spoke her name. Trembling with fear she sprang from her bed and came out to meet him.

BACK TO THE BUNGALOW.

The moonlight made her pale face so white that it seemed almost like a ghost, and he could hardly speak. He tried to tell her gently, but before he had half-finished she fell fainting at his feet.

A native servant took her in his stalwart arms, and by torchlight carried her the ten miles back to the trader's bungalow, while Roy and Scott and the Russians followed close behind.

"Those little birds were not so far from right, Scott," Roy said as they walked along.

"Well, at any rate. I'm glad we didn't have anything to do with his

"HE WAS MY FATHER."

death. I hope there was nothing about it for which we can be responsible," Scott replied.

"Responsible?" said Roy, "why, Scott! Did you not risk your life to save him?"

"I wish that I had saved him," Scott answered.

Neither of the boys saw Louise that night. She was taken into the bungalow at once and given in charge of one of the women servants.

In the morning the Russians went to her and told her the whole story. Then she asked for Roy and Scott, and they were conducted to her room.

For a moment no one spoke. She was trembling still, and her cheeks were flushed with crying. She looked from one to the other with pleading eyes, then bursting into tears fell upon her knees beside a little bench before the window, sobbing:

"He was my father! yes, he was my father!"

They lost no time in reaching the coast, and setting sail for Australia, where the treasure which Captain Downing had taken from Sebastopol had been forwarded.

Louise accompanied them, under the care of an American lady whose husband had recently died at Rajok, and who was very anxious to secure a passage home again for herself and a little daughter.

The Russian officer suggested that at Australia he and the ladies should take a steamer for quicker passage, if they desired, but Louise stubbornly declared that she wanted no steamer and wanted no strangers.

"I want to stay on the *Snowbird*," she said, "and go at once to Vera. I want to tell her how I have wronged her; and take her at once to that beautiful home in Sebastopol."

So it was decided that they should all go together.

CHAPTER XVI.

THE LAST VOYAGE.

THROUGH storm and sunshine, in fair weather and foul, the white wings of the *Snowbird* caught the breeze, leaping, flying over the waves. They stopped at Sydney, Australia, only long enough to refit and restock for the voyage home, as the Russians at once received orders to secure the treasure and return to Russia, by way of America, with the rightful heir. Steadily onward she kept her course, whatever the weather till the huge albatross swept through the air about her and they sighted the solitary cone rising out of the waves, south of the southern point of South America. Rounding Cape Horn, they turned northward from the cold south seas, where winter was beginning to show itself while summer was upon the threshold at the North.

"Scott," said Roy, " do you realize that we are as near the south pole as we were to the north pole when we were half-way between Newfoundland and Greenland ? "

" Well, does it seem to you as though we were the same two individuals who guided this craft through those ice-fields ? " Scott replied.

Thus far they had enjoyed a delightful voyage, with very little monotony, though it had already been over six weeks in length. The three passengers were a wonderful addition, and with so many hands to help in running the *Snowbird* there was very little work for any one to do.

After they passed the snow-covered mountains of Tierra del

Fuego, and, through the glass, took a good look at the town that lies nearest the south pole, recall ng their visit to Hammerfest, lying nearest the north pole, Roy and Scott became more serious, and spent more time in elaborate calculations and estimates over the charts.

"We've been within twenty degrees of the north pole and within thirty-five of the south pole," said Roy; "almost round the world from

THE ALBATROSS.

north to south, and quite round it from west to east. But I tell you we've got a blessed doubtful job ahead of us."

"O, Roy! you're always looking on the dark side," Scott exclaimed. "Say we fall off to six knots and stop a day at Rio Janeiro, we shall still have four days, five hours, forty-eight minutes and fifty seconds grace, allowing for three days before sailing."

"Well, that's coming pretty close on a nine thousand mile home run," said Roy. "We are likely to lie in a dead calm for a month or be blown back a thousand miles n a gale, so we'd better not set our hopes too high."

"I'll bet you we can do it, unless we split a rock somewhere on the way." said Scott, banging the table.

The captain had been a si ent listener. Now he said:

"It takes the man who has confidence to accomplish anything. I confess I'm doubtful about it, as Roy is, and if he'll consent I think the best thing is to give Scott command for the rest of the voyage."

" That's a good idea," Roy exclaimed.

" I'll do the best I can," said Scott, " if you two will be an advising committee and speak up, right honest, all the time."

" You bet we will," said Roy. " We're quite as anxious as you are to see you win."

So it was arranged.

The first drawback appeared almost instantly, in the force against them of the Brazilian current. The next followed close upon it in a steady head wind, and they were forced to tack and make only five knots an hour at that.

The mountain peaks of Rio Janeiro appeared, at last, with clouds circling their summits, but they had lost three days of their surplus when they entered the harbor and waited only long enough to fill the water-tanks and lay in a supply of fruit, fresh meat and vegetables.

Rio was a beautiful city, and they had been on board the *Snowbird* for sixty-nine days, but all were in haste to be onward bound, and they would not have stopped at all had it not been that their fresh water gave out three days before. They had bathed in salt water, and for cooking and drinking the cook had " boiled the ocean and landed the steam," as Scott expressed it.

" We've only one day of grace left, have we, over a six knots an hour average ? " Roy asked as they left Rio behind them.

" One day, five hours, forty-eight minutes and fifty seconds, Roy," Scott replied. " And one day more, for the dates on those Rio papers reminded me that in going round the world to the east we had gained a day. It's really yesterday. See ? "

CAPE HORN.

Slowly they worked their way up to Cape St. Roque, losing three days more.

THE JANGADA RACE.

Just before they reached the cape they passed three jangadas in an exciting race. They were native rafts, of the most clumsy construction, into which enormous sails had been rigged, with two Indians upon each jangada, to pull upon a rope attached to a post, and act as ballast, while

A GLIMPSE OF THE GULF OF MEXICO.

a party of gentlemen manned the rafts and enjoyed themselves hugely.

"If we were only going their way we could make ten knots an hour," Roy muttered.

"When we round the cape it will be better," Scott replied, and it certainly was better. They ran at once into the equatorial current, which was in their favor, and a good breeze from the starboard beam.

All the spirits on board rose with the good fortune, and there was merriment enough till they plunged into the yellow water which is thrown far into the ocean by the great Amazon. There the wind died out and they began to drift, with the sails flapping against the mast.

"We'd made a whole day back again," Scott remarked reproachfully.

"Which leaves us again five hours and forty-eight minutes "—

"And fifty seconds, Roy. For mercy's sake, give us all that belongs to us," Scott interrupted with a laugh.

They made slow progress through the islands guarding the Gulf of Mexico, sometimes drifting along within a hundred feet of them. It gave them many a glimpse of the most picturesque of tropical scenery, and groups of natives, half-Spanish, half-Indian, gathered upon the shore, but nothing aroused Scott's enthusiasm so thoroughly as a murky, yellow cloud which lay one night along the western horizon.

"That means wind, or I'm an Esquimau," he exclaimed.

"The glass has been falling all day. I'm afraid it means too much wind," replied the Russian captain.

He was right. A tornado struck them about midnight. One sail was torn to shreds and a jib carried away before a hand could be lifted.

The *Snowbird* reeled, careened and for a moment seemed slowly bending to the furious gale and doomed to capsize.

Scott was on deck in an instant. She was slowly pulling herself out of the water. It was a moment of intense excitement, but she righted at last.

"Shall we take in sail?" Roy asked.

"Not a stitch!" Scott replied, as he grasped the helm and brought her back to due north.

"The wind will do it if we don't," said the Russian.

"Well, I'm going to make the most of them till it does, if she can keep her nose out of water," Scott muttered. "Call up all hands and set two lookouts. We're just bowling."

A sailor lashed himself to the masthead. The Russian clung to life ropes in the prow and Roy stood braced against the mast, while Scott with a sailor to help him clutched the helm which was sometimes more than both of them could manage.

Thus the *Snowbird* held her course steadily northward, while she drifted broadside to the west, under pressure of the heavy seas, through the most terrible night which the boys had ever witnessed. More than once Scott was swept from his feet and hung at arms-length from the helm as the *Snowbird* lay over almost to the rail and the big chasers made a clean dash over the deck; but she was light and strong and fought her way almost like something that was alive.